From the Casefiles of Shelby Woo

THE CRIME: Red Sox star outfielder Ricky Baines has been victimized by a string of unlucky occurrences. Now his whole baseball career is in trouble!

THE QUESTION: Who would sabotage Ricky—and why?

THE SUSPECTS: *Ruth Williams*—a sports reporter who scoops everyone with her coverage of Baines and his troubles. Is this the result of hard work, or has she been manufacturing the story for her own gain?
Tom Van Ness—the starting left fielder before Baines came along. Could he be ensuring that he doesn't finish his career on the bench?
Bobby Pesky—he has the biggest memorabilia collection in town *and* a grudge against Ricky Baines.

COMPLICATIONS: Why would someone go to all this trouble to harm Ricky? Shelby is baffled. But with Vince and Angie on her team, she's hoping to hit upon a grand-slam clue!

The Mystery Files of Shelby Woo™

Available from MINSTREL Books

THE GREEN MONSTER

JAMES PONTI

A
MINSTREL®
BOOK

Published by POCKET BOOKS
New York   London   Toronto   Sydney   Tokyo   Singapore

This book is a work of fiction. Names, characters, places and incidents are products of the author's imagination or are used fictitiously. Any resemblance to actual events or locales or persons, living or dead, is entirely coincidental.

A MINSTREL PAPERBACK *Original*

A Minstrel Book published by
POCKET BOOKS, a division of Simon & Schuster Inc.
1230 Avenue of the Americas, New York, NY 10020

ISBN: 0-671-02696-8

First Minstrel Books printing April 1999

10 9 8 7 6 5 4 3 2 1

Front cover photo by Pat Hill Studio

Printed in the U.S.A.

For my mother,
who taught me how to write

THE GREEN MONSTER

Chapter

1

The more I try to organize my life, the less control I seem to have over it. It used to bother me; but I'm beginning to think it might be a good thing. After all, what fun would life be if everything happened exactly the way you had it written out in your Day Planner? You need a good surprise every now and then.

This past year has been full of surprises. When I first moved to Wilton, Massachusetts, I hated it. I missed my friends in Florida. I missed walking on the sand along the beach. And I actually had dreams about the chili fries they serve at C.J.'s.

But now I love it here. I've made great friends. I discovered it's just as much fun to walk in the snow. And although he hasn't perfected the chili fries yet, the cook at Fanny's does whip up a mean plate of nachos.

The friends, though, were the biggest surprise. Vince and Angie are the best. I can't imagine not having met them. Vince has turned out to be more than a friend. I guess we're boyfriend and girlfriend. We've talked about it some. It's not official, but we are going to Spring Fling together.

As for Angie, she's nothing but surprises. I mean, this is a girl who is brilliant in every way. She's won the school science fair two years in a row. She can tell you anything about physics or chemistry. Yet, somehow, she actually believes the Boston Red Sox play better if she watches them while clutching her lucky pillow. Not that it looks much like a pillow anymore. It's just this mangled purple blob.

Angie's not alone. It seems like everyone believes in some sort of good luck charm. I came across a lot of them on the last case I solved. Unlike most of the mysteries I take on, this one didn't start in the middle of the night with some criminal cracking the combination to a safe. It started in between fourth and fifth periods with Angie dialing the combination to her locker. It's a case I call The Green Monster. Good luck solving it before the tardy bell rings.

Within seconds of the bell sounding, the hallways of Wilton Patriot High School were flooded with students. Shelby Woo and Angie Burns had to fight a tide of hungry lunch-bound seniors just to make it from English class to their lockers.

"I should have known better than to come to school on Friday the thirteenth," Angie exclaimed as she expertly weaved through the crowd.

"What does the date have to do with anything?" Shelby asked. Just then she had to take a quick step backward to avoid getting squished between two passing football players.

Angie had reached her locker and was starting to spin the dial on the combination lock. "Friday the thirteenth's bad luck," she said. "Everybody knows that." She gave Shelby a "duh" look.

Shelby shot one right back at her. "I know some people believe that," she replied. "But not you. Aren't you the goddess of logic and reason?"

"Logic and reason don't explain Mr. Allen's giving a killer test that I completely forgot to study for."

"Yeah. What was that about?" Shelby asked. "I mean, who knows the meaning of the word *moira*?"

"It's a Greek term for destiny," Angie rattled off. "It has to do with the fate of the protagonist."

Shelby couldn't believe it. "I thought you didn't study," she said, more than a little peeved.

"I didn't," Angie answered. "I just got lucky on that one."

"Yeah, it was *lucky* you knew some obscure Greek literary term." Shelby just shook her head. "So help me, Angie. If you aced this test . . ." Shelby took a deep breath, and her expression soured instantly. "What *is* that smell?"

Angie sniffed. "Well, they're dissecting frogs in biology this week. It could be formaldehyde.

4

But then again, it is sloppy-joe day in the cafeteria, so it's a toss-up."

The two girls thought about this for a moment. "We've got to start eating off campus," Shelby said.

Angie nodded in agreement and reached for her chemistry book. When she pulled it from the locker shelf, she knocked a folded piece of paper onto the floor.

It was a note addressed simply to "A.B." She opened it and read it aloud.

> "Roses are red
> Violets are blue
> Don't tell anyone, but
> I've got a crush on you. . . ."

Angie's voice trailed off as she read the last line. The note had caught her completely off guard. In an instant, she forgot about the test. She forgot about the students' pushing and shoving their way to class. She even forgot about the horrible smell. (Well, she would have forgotten about the horrible smell if it hadn't been quite so bad.) She just stared down at the paper and silently reread it.

> Don't tell anyone, but
> I've got a crush on you.

"You've got a secret admirer," Shelby teased, a broad grin stretching across her face.

"No, I don't." Angie tried to play it cool. "It's probably just a joke. Besides, it's way corny."

"Not corny," corrected Shelby. "Cute." She quickly scanned the hallway looking for possible candidates. Suddenly every guy looked different. Any one of them might be *the* guy for Angie. "Who do you think sent it?"

Angie couldn't admit that she had already started making a mental list of possible candidates. And she also couldn't admit that she was organizing that list into two categories: Dreamy and Dreary. She was determined to play it cool. "Who cares?" She tossed the note back into her locker.

"I care," protested Shelby as she grabbed it.

"And so do you." The warning bell rang. Now they really had to hurry. Shelby stuck the note in her pocket.

"Hey, what are you doing with my note?" Angie asked.

"I'm going to figure out who wrote it," Shelby said. "After all, I am a detective."

"I believe the nameplate on your desk says 'intern,'" Angie corrected.

"'Administrative assistant to the head of the detective division,'" Shelby responded with a flourish of pride. "Trust me. I'll have your case solved by the end of the day." With that, they rushed off to their respective classes.

In truth, Angie cared a lot. She'd gone out on a few dates but had never had what she considered a real boyfriend. She was always the girl boys talked to about their problems with other girls. She had always thought it was because she was a little awkward and brainy. But Shelby was a little awkward and brainy, too, and she had hit it off with Vince in no time flat.

Just when she had come to accept the fact that she would never have a boyfriend, she discovered someone had a crush on her. She was thrilled. But at the same time, she couldn't help but expect it all to turn out badly. In short, she was a total wreck.

Shelby, meanwhile, was determined to learn the guy's identity. She had always figured the boys at Wilton were morons for not chasing after Angie anyway. How could they miss all she had to offer? Shelby couldn't wait to figure out which one of them had finally gotten a clue.

She spent all of algebra and most of American history scouring the note for clues. Despite her bold predictions, she was nowhere near having it solved by the time she met Angie in the student parking lot after school.

"All right," Angie asked, "who's my Romeo?"

Shelby cringed. "I'm afraid it's going to take a little more time than I first thought."

"Just as I expected," Angie replied. "An intern by any other name is still an intern."

Even though Angie was kidding, Shelby felt the need to defend her skills as a detective. "I may not know his name, but I *can* describe him for you."

Angie gave her a skeptical look.

"He's tall, creative, and is deeply concerned about the environment," Shelby said confidently.

"I'm also leaning toward cute and hopelessly romantic, but those are just hunches."

"And you got this from what?" Angie asked. "The little detective fairy that sings to you from your shoulder?"

"Standard Operating Procedure." Shelby drew out each word for emphasis. "When searching for a perp, you've got to do a profile based on the information at hand."

"So now he's a perp?" Angie couldn't help laughing whenever Shelby used tough-cop lingo.

"Look at this paper," Shelby said, pointing to a green recycling logo on the bottom of the page. "It's recycled. That means he must be concerned about the environment."

"It could mean he's a big bully who steals notebooks from people who are concerned about the environment," said Angie.

Shelby ignored her and kept going. "Now check out his handwriting."

"You mean his incredibly messy handwriting?" Angie said.

"It's a classic sign of creativity."

"It's a classic sign of messiness." Angie pointed to a greasy smudge on the corner of the sheet. "Extreme messiness. Does your profile have him living in the auto shop?"

"Laugh all you want," Shelby said. "You're looking at solid detective work here."

"And you think he's tall because—why?" Angie could hardly wait to hear Shelby's reasoning. "You measured the angle of the handwriting and calculated the length of his arm?"

"No," Shelby said proudly. "The note was on top of the books in your locker. That means the secret admirer slid it through the slats up high and not down low."

As much as she hated to admit it, this made sense to Angie. She especially hated to admit it after she ran through her mental list again. None of the tall guys were on the Dreamy side.

"How's it going?" Vince said cheerily. He gave Shelby a quick but sweet kiss on the cheek.

"Great for Shelby," Angie said. "I, on the other hand, am completely miserable." She slumped against the trunk of her car.

"She got a letter from a secret admirer," Shelby explained.

"Isn't that good?" asked Vince.

"Not if the guy's some freakishly tall slob who steals notebooks from ecologically conscious kids."

Shelby tried to insert a little optimism. "We don't know that he's 'freakishly' tall. He may just be above average."

"I bet you know who sent it, don't you, Vince?" Angie looked him dead in the eye. "Go ahead. Break it to me."

"How would I know?" Vince asked incredulously.

"You're a guy," Angie said. "Don't you all talk?"

"Yeah. Right after lunch," Vince answered. "We all get together, hug, and tell each other who we have crushes on. But we're sworn to secrecy."

Shelby slugged him in the shoulder.

"Ow. What was that for?" he asked.

"Unnecessary sarcasm," Shelby told him. "We've got a friend in pain, and you're not helping."

"Okay, I'm sorry," Vince told Angie. "I don't know who wrote it. But I bet it's someone great."

"You think so?" asked Angie.

"Sure. Look at you. You're nice. You're smart. You're tons of fun to be with. What guy wouldn't want to go out with you?"

Shelby slugged him in the shoulder again.

"Double ow. What was *that* for?" Vince asked.

"For never saying nice stuff like that about me," Shelby told him.

"Before I have to visit the school nurse," Vince said, rubbing his shoulder, "do you equally attractive and appealing girls have anything planned for tonight?"

He reached into his pocket and pulled out three tickets. "Red Sox–Yankees, seven o'clock at Fenway."

In an instant, Angie filed "The Case of the Secret Admirer" away in the back of her mind. "Okay, *miserable* is gone and I am now officially jazzed. How'd you score Sox–Yankees tickets?"

"My brother couldn't use them so he gave them to me."

Angie could barely contain her excitement. With the exception of science, she had no greater passion in life than the Boston Red Sox. She had been a die-hard fan ever since she was a little girl and went to her first game with her dad.

"Great," Shelby said. She had never been to a Red Sox game, or any other major-league baseball game for that matter.

A few hours later they were on their way to the stadium. Angie spent most of the drive into town telling Shelby names and numbers that Shelby knew she would never remember. Angie was deep into explaining the intricacies of the infield-fly rule when she missed the stadium parking lot.

"Weren't you supposed to turn back there?" Shelby asked, pointing down a street that led to Fenway Park.

"Yes," Angie replied as she kept going the wrong way, "but the last time I came, I made this same mis-turn."

"And?" Shelby said, hoping there was more to the story.

"And . . . the Sox beat the Blue Jays seven–O." Angie said it as if this reasoning made total sense. "It's good luck."

"Again with the luck." It would just never make sense to Shelby that someone so dedicated to science could put so much faith in something as illogical as luck.

"Shelby," Angie replied, "you don't understand the role that luck plays in baseball. Especially with the Red Sox. They need all the help they can get."

Angie was not alone in these beliefs. The Red Sox had a long history of seeming unbeatable at the start of a season, only to lose at the end. Most of the team's fans attributed this to the fact that Fenway Park had opened the same week the seemingly unsinkable *Titanic* plunged to the ocean floor in April 1912.

"Where are our seats?" Angie asked as they walked to the ballpark along Landsdowne Street.

"Down the foul line in left," Vince answered.

"That's great. We'll have a perfect view of the Green Monster." Angie was getting more excited with each step.

"What's the Green Monster?" Shelby asked in all sincerity.

Angie stopped cold. "You don't know what the Green Monster is?"

Shelby could tell that this fact amazed Angie. "Should I?" she asked. She couldn't even imagine what a Green Monster might be.

"It's the left-field wall," Vince explained.

"This road we're on—Landsdowne—was already here when they built the park. So they had to make the wall closer to home plate than it should have been. To make up for it, they made it really tall. And, since it's green, everyone calls it the Green Monster."

"Neat," Shelby said unconvincingly. *First Greek literary terms, now baseball nicknames*, she thought to herself. *Whatever happened to learning state capitals?*

Angie was especially excited because they'd have a great vantage point to watch her favorite player— left fielder Ricky Baines. Baines had been struggling lately, and to help him out of his slump, Angie had brought along a host of good luck charms. Among them was the wrapper from the gum she had nervously chewed the night the Sox last made the playoffs, as well as a quarter that former Red Sox pitching great Roger Clemens had dropped at a movie theater Angie had been at, too.

They took their seats just as the Red Sox ran from the dugout onto the field.

"Perfect timing," said Vince.

"Which one's Ricky Baines?" Shelby asked.

"He's in left field," Angie said, gesturing

toward the Green Monster. "Wait a minute. That's not him. . . ." Angie couldn't think of a single reason for Baines's being left out of the lineup. She wondered if he had been injured.

Next to her, a man was listening to the broadcast of the game on a small radio. That's how they heard the news from the announcer.

Ricky Baines had disappeared!

Chapter
2

According to the announcer, the Red Sox had no idea why Baines was missing. Still, they didn't sound alarmed. They explained that over the course of a 162-game season, it was inevitable that one or two players would miss showing up for a game. They told the story of a Braves pitcher who got lost on the Georgia interstate and spent four hours driving through Atlanta desperately searching for the stadium. They told another one about a couple of Red Sox players who once jumped off a team bus stuck in a traffic jam only to be found at the airport three days later trying to leave the country.

Although the announcers were laughing about the anecdotes, Angie was concerned.

"Considering Ricky grew up in Boston," she said, "I doubt he got lost on the way to the park. And from what I've seen, he isn't exactly the type to try to hop a plane out of the country."

The whole thing sparked Shelby's natural curiosity. "Who's that playing for him?" she asked.

"Tom Van Ness," answered Angie. "He used to be pretty good. I think he made the All-Star team when he played for the Twins."

Shelby flipped through Angie's souvenir program and saw that Van Ness had played for four different teams during his ten years in the major leagues. He had signed with the Red Sox expecting to be their starting left fielder for the last few years of his career.

Ricky Baines had changed all that. Ricky's sudden arrival and instant stardom had moved Tom out of left field and onto the bench. Angie felt pretty certain this would be his last year with the Sox. "I think the only reason they kept him was to help Ricky learn the ropes," she added.

Angie was right. The two players had lockers next to each other's because the coaches wanted them to spend as much time together as possible. A young player like Ricky could learn a lot from an experienced one like Tom.

Shelby couldn't help it. She started thinking about this as if it were a case. She wasn't alone. As word of Ricky's no-show spread throughout the ballpark, the fans began to develop theories of their own.

Some reasoned that it was a publicity stunt designed to generate interest in the team. Others were certain it was an attempt by Baines to get the Red Sox to renegotiate his contract. Angie almost got into an argument with one creep who said, "I don't care why, I'm just glad the bum is gone."

Not one of the 34,218 fans in the ballpark, however, guessed that Ricky was just a mile away sitting in the kitchen of his mother's house eating a giant plate of spaghetti and meatballs.

For Ricky, however, it made perfect sense. Whenever things went wrong, he went straight to his mother's. After all, he was just twenty-one, barely out of high school. And, unlike everyone else, his mother didn't treat him like "Ricky the baseball star." She treated him as she had when he was twelve years old and nobody had heard of him. She even made him do the dishes when he was done eating.

Fame had come suddenly. The previous season, Ricky had been named the American League Rookie of the Year and became the instant darling of hometown fans. With that, however, came great expectations for the future.

Despite flashes of brilliance, Ricky had been struggling during the beginning of his second season. The coaches told him not to worry. They were certain he would snap out of it. But Ricky felt as if he was letting everybody down. Worse, though, was the bad luck.

Like many ballplayers, Ricky was incredibly superstitious: When he got dressed for a game, he put on his right sock and cleat before his left. He always listened to the same CD on his headphones in the clubhouse. And he always wore a Roxbury High T-shirt under his jersey.

Lately his superstitions had been working against him. He had been haunted by a seemingly endless series of bad omens and unlucky coincidences. For example, most players change caps throughout the season. Ricky, though, broke in a new one on opening day and wore it all season long. During a recent road trip to Kansas City, his cap had disappeared. That night, he'd committed a pair of errors that had cost Boston the game.

Last week the bat he had used since coming up from the minors splintered during a crucial game. He struck out three straight times with his new bat. Two of the strikeouts occurred in situations in which he might have won the game.

The final blow had occurred earlier that afternoon. Already nervous because it was Friday the 13th, Ricky was taking a shower when a mirror fell off his bedroom wall and shattered on the floor.

The mixed omens of a broken mirror and Friday the 13th made him decide he couldn't play. He was certain that he would do something wrong and cost the team the game. He drove to Fenway Park, but when he got there, he just kept going to his mother's house.

He missed a great game. In the bottom of the ninth, the Red Sox were down by a run when Tom Van Ness came up to bat. Shelby was surprised at how much she was caught up in the action. She looked down and noticed Angie nervously rubbing her lucky Roger Clemens quarter as Van Ness swung and missed the first pitch. Suddenly Angie's good luck charms didn't seem quite so silly to Shelby. She wanted Van Ness to connect.

"Where's that gum wrapper?" Shelby asked. Angie smiled and dug it out of her pocket. Shelby gripped it as tightly as she could. It worked.

Van Ness drilled the next pitch deep into left field. Shelby, Angie, and Vince had the perfect seats to see the ball carom off the Green Monster and bounce past the outfielder. By the time the Yankees got the ball, Van Ness was standing on second, and two Boston runners had scored. The game was over. The Red Sox had won, and Shelby was hooked on both the sport and the team. The crowd cheered wildly for Van Ness as he jogged off the field.

Ricky Baines watched it all on television. As the fans cheered his replacement, he was more certain than ever that he had done the right thing.

"If that had been me," he said to his worried

mother, "I would have struck out and we would have lost."

Angie, meanwhile, was trying to pull into the slow crawl of cars that surrounded Fenway Park.

"Thanks so much for the tickets," she said to Vince.

"Yeah," added Shelby. "It was great."

"Except for the part about Ricky Baines," he said. "That's too weird."

Angie fiddled with the radio, trying to get the postgame wrap-up. Angie's car stereo being what it was, it was hard to hear the announcer through all the static.

The announcer said that Red Sox officials had spoken with Baines by telephone and wanted all the listeners and fans to know that he was all right. "According to the team," the announcer said, "Ricky missed the game for an unspecified family matter."

There were no details beyond that. Angie still thought it was strange. " 'Unspecified family matter' usually means they don't want to say what really happened," she said.

Next the announcer interviewed Tom Van Ness, who modestly said that he had been lucky to get the right hit at the right time. He also expressed concern for Baines.

"Ricky's having some rough times right now," Van Ness said. "We've got to help him win back his confidence. Ricky's like a younger brother. We care about him."

"See?" Angie said knowingly. "A second ago it was an 'unspecified family matter.' Now it's rough times and no confidence. There's more there than they're telling us."

The radio cut to a commercial, and Shelby turned the volume down. She wanted to know more about Baines. "Not baseball stuff," she said. "What kind of guy is he?"

Angie eased the car onto the expressway and headed toward Wilton. "My cousin Marie went to high school with him in Roxbury," Angie said. "She says he was one of the nicest guys she knew. I also read that even though he makes a lot of money playing baseball, he goes to college during the off-season."

"I read that," Vince chimed in from the back-seat. "He promised his mom he'd get a degree."

Shelby was beginning to like Ricky Baines.

"The best thing about him is that he doesn't

charge for autographs," Angie said. "He stays after the games and signs them for free."

"I hope he's all right," Shelby said. "He sounds like a pretty decent guy."

It was almost midnight when Angie dropped Shelby off at her grandfather's bed-and-breakfast. "See you in the morning," Angie said.

"Don't remind me," a drowsy Shelby replied.

Angie was glad to see her father still awake when she got home a few minutes later. She loved to dissect the games with him. He listened with rapt attention as she filled him in on all the details of the game. This was the real appeal of the Red Sox for Angie. She wasn't really that much of a sports fan. She liked the Red Sox as much as she did because it was something she shared with her father.

One of her fondest memories was when her father had woken her up so that she could watch a replay of Dave Henderson hitting a dramatic home run that helped send the Red Sox to the World Series. She was six years old, and she had sat on his lap beaming as they watched the play over and over.

That night they talked about the mystery of Ricky Baines. Like Angie, he suspected that there was more to the story than they were being told.

Angie kissed her father good night and went up to bed. She rushed through her nightly routine: twenty sit-ups, wash face, check e-mail. Within minutes she was snug in her bed—but she couldn't sleep. She rolled over and opened the drawer on her nightstand. She pulled out a piece of paper. It was the note from her secret admirer.

She hadn't brought it up once all night, but it had been on her mind every minute. She reread it one more time.

Who are you, mystery guy?

Chapter

3

Shelby loved the concept of volunteerism. She thought it was great that kids her age were trying to make the world a better place. She just wasn't thrilled with the idea of getting up at the crack of dawn to do it.

Why can't the world be saved in the afternoon? she thought as she groggily poured herself a bowl of cereal. Eating it sapped what little strength she had at that hour. She battled to stay awake.

It was somewhere during the third spoonful that she decided she was fully capable of eating cornflakes with her eyes shut. "How hard can it be?" she reasoned. After two "blind" bites, during which she only spilled a little milk, she convinced herself that she was fully capable of eating cornflakes with her eyes closed *and* her head resting against the kitchen table.

She never made it to her sixth bite.

When Angie found her, Shelby was fast asleep, her face just inches from the bowl. Amazingly, the spoon in her hand was perfectly balanced and still held milk and cereal.

"Wake up," Angie said as she gently shook Shelby's shoulder. "We don't want to be late."

Shelby moved only those muscles absolutely necessary to speak. "It's impossible to be late this early in the morning." She momentarily perked up to make a point. "Besides, you're the one who kept me up till midnight with your baseball game."

With some prodding, Shelby managed to make it to the front seat of Angie's car. There she sneaked an extra twenty minutes of sleep while they drove down to the Boston Harbor area.

"Look," Angie said, pointing toward an old-fashioned boat docked nearby. "This is where the Boston Tea Party took place." For some reason, Angie seemed to think that a little history lesson might liven Shelby up.

"They were smart," Shelby said of the patriots whose protest was a key moment during the American Revolution. "They saved the world at night."

Shelby finally began to wake up as they walked along Museum Wharf. The damp, cool wind blowing in her face might have had something to do with her sudden alertness.

"How'd I ever let you talk me into this?" Shelby asked as they hurried up the steps to the Computer Museum. The "this" in question was a mentoring program. Twenty-five high school students from Wilton Patriot had volunteered to spend three Saturday mornings at the museum teaching elementary-school kids about computers.

Jerry Hubbs, the president of the school's computer club, had come up with the idea. He convinced the museum, which was one of the most popular attractions in all of Boston, to open its doors two hours early to the volunteers and a busload of third-graders.

The smiles on the faces of the eight-year-olds were all it took. Shelby perked right up when she saw them. "Now I remember how you talked me into it," she said to Angie.

For the first ten minutes the class listened—and laughed—as Jerry and his friend Scott Bushnell did a demonstration at the Walk Through Computer. This was an actual working computer that was big enough to go inside. It had a giant keyboard and mouse—both of which worked—and a monitor that was twelve feet high.

The demonstration was just silly enough to get everybody in a good mood. Jerry kept sneezing and saying it was because he had a computer virus. Scott turned into a superhero called Mega-Byte and saved the day. Shelby was impressed by how funny her two schoolmates were. When they finished, the group broke up into smaller groups. The high schoolers were split up into pairs, each pair being assigned to a different exhibit.

Shelby and Angie were stationed at an exhibit about the Internet. Angie did most of the talking, while Shelby sniffed out the shy ones. After all, Jerry's one instruction had been "Make sure all the kids get involved."

Shelby was particularly drawn to one kid in

the back of the group. He had a tough-guy act going, but Shelby could tell it was all show. She tried to be a good detective and figure a way to break the ice with him.

Her answer came from the Red Sox cap he had pulled down over his eyes. She walked over and stood next to him for about a minute. She waited for a lull in what Angie was saying, and then she set the trap.

"Did you see the game last night?" she asked.

"What?" He looked around, not sure if she was talking to him.

"Red Sox–Yankees. It was great. I was sitting right by the Green Monster." Shelby said it matter-of-factly, as if she never missed a game.

"You were there?" he asked. Shelby could tell by his eyes that she had him interested.

"Yeah," she said, trying not to sound too eager. "I wonder what's up with Ricky Baines. That's pretty weird, not showing up like that."

"I wish I knew. Ricky's my favorite player."

"Mine, too," she said. She had him hooked; now it was time to reel him in. "Let's find out."

She went over to an open computer terminal. "What's your name?"

"Nate." Before Nate knew what was happening, Shelby had him logged in on the Internet. She clicked on a search engine.

"What are you doing?" Nate asked.

"*We're* searching the Internet to see if there's anything on it about Ricky missing the game." She typed "Ricky Baines AND missing" and hit the search button. After a few moments the screen was filled with possible links.

"Check it out." Nate couldn't believe the gobs of information that appeared on the screen. Instinctively, he took a step closer to the computer.

Shelby clicked on a link that led to the website of the *Boston Beacon.* Saturday's sports page came up on the screen, which instantly filled with pictures, statistics, and articles about the previous night's game. Nate couldn't wait to get on the keyboard himself.

Shelby was thrilled by his reaction. She showed him the basics and told him she'd be right there to answer any questions. She even showed him how to print a file. She clicked on the lead story, and within seconds it was coming out on the printer next to them.

"That is so cool." Nate took the keyboard and

never looked back. Shelby felt great. While she waited to make sure Nate had it all down, she flipped through the article she had printed.

SLUMPING STAR STIFFS SOX
by Ruth Williams of the *Beacon* Staff

Troubled left fielder Ricky Baines made it home last night. He just didn't make it to home plate. While his teammates were battling the New York Yankees, Baines was eating spaghetti in his mother's kitchen and watching the game on television. . . .

The article continued on about the accidents and omens that had been distracting Baines. Shelby reread the article carefully. A missing hat, a broken bat, a shattered mirror. She just didn't believe it could all be coincidence. She wondered if something or someone else was behind Ricky's run of bad luck.

Angie, meanwhile, was having some bad luck herself while demonstrating how to use e-mail for a half dozen third-graders. With all of them looking over her shoulder, she went to her e-mail box and opened a letter that she thought was

33

from a friend. It turned out to be from the secret admirer.

> I think you're the best
> We'd have lots of fun
> I hope you're not going
> out with someone

Angie probably would have liked the poem if she had been alone. But it wasn't exactly what she wanted a group of eight-year-olds to see. Before she could wipe the screen clear, they were already chanting about Angie and her boyfriend "sittin' in a tree, K-I-S-S-I-N-G." This was especially troubling to one little guy who had already developed an instant crush on her.

"It had to be me!" Angie wailed to Shelby after the kids had moved on to the next exhibit. "Only I could have something so embarrassing happen."

While they waited for the next group to arrive, Shelby got back on-line and reopened Angie's letter.

"What are you doing?" Angie asked. "Trying to make a fool out of me in front of a whole new group of eight-year-olds?"

"No. I'm trying to get a return address from

that letter," said Shelby. She checked out the path the letter had taken through cyberspace. "Well, what do you know?"

"What? What?" Angie asked excitedly.

"The letter was sent from a computer in this museum."

"What does that mean?" Angie wondered.

"I think it means that your secret admirer is one of the guys in the group." Shelby was thinking fast. "We've just got to figure out which one."

Just then the next group of third-graders entered. Angie quickly closed the letter and began to talk. Meanwhile, Shelby did some quick math in her head. Of the twenty-five volunteers, there were twelve boys. She was certain the secret admirer had to be one of them. She knew that two of the guys had girlfriends. That left ten.

Shelby knew that Angie was impatient. *This whole secret admirer thing must be making her mental,* she thought. *I'll tell her to trust her "moira." I still don't know what it means. But it sounds good.*

When the morning session came to an end, all of the third-graders headed back to their bus. Nate made a point of getting Shelby's attention and waving goodbye to her.

Once they were gone, all the volunteers got together for a recap in a museum meeting room. Jerry thanked everyone for coming and handed each of them a short form to fill out. Shelby and Angie bagged the form and used the time to consider each guy in the group. They had the list narrowed down to ten. There was still work to do.

"Too cute," Angie said, explaining why one wouldn't be interested in her.

"I know for a fact he hates me," she said about another.

Within a few minutes, Angie had narrowed the list all the way down to zero. "It's none of these guys," she said with great certainty.

"Well, according to the date and time on the e-mail, it was sent today," said Shelby. "Which means it has to be one of these guys."

Angie scanned their faces once again. "Maybe it's one of the third-graders."

Just then, for no apparent reason, Shelby bolted up and blurted, "Angie and I are going out to lunch if anyone wants to come along."

"We are?" Angie had no idea what Shelby was talking about. This, in itself, was not an unusual occurrence. But Angie had only two dollars on her. She hadn't planned on eating out.

Sitting back down, Shelby quickly and quietly explained that there was no way the secret admirer would pass up such an easy opportunity to spend time with her. This made sense to Angie. Suddenly Angie decided she could eat rather well on two dollars.

"Yeah, we're going out," Angie announced a little more forcefully than she had intended. "Just not someplace too expensive."

They ate at a snack bar shaped like a giant milk bottle right there on the wharf. They sat at picnic tables overlooking Boston Harbor.

Three guys joined the group—Jerry, Scott, and another computer clubber named Nonito Marchan. All three were about the same height, so Shelby's profile wasn't any help.

Jerry was a senior and planned to go to the University of Connecticut the next year. In addition to being president of the computer club, he played on the school tennis team.

Scott was in Mr. Allen's class with Shelby and Angie. He was always cutting up in class. Once, when Mr. Allen left class a few minutes early,

Scott hopped up and stole his podium. He held the podium hostage for three days, leaving rhyming ransom notes on Mr. Allen's desk. The teacher was so impressed with the prank that he raised Scott's grade a full letter.

Nonito, though, was a complete unknown. He had gone to their school for only a few months, having moved to Wilton with his mother after his parents got divorced.

None of the three had been in the room when Angie had accidentally opened the e-mail. Shelby hoped that whoever sent it didn't know Angie had read it already.

With her two dollars, Angie had enough money for a corn dog and a small soda. A very small soda. She sat down and tried not to think about her secret admirer. If Shelby was right, he was one of the three guys at the table.

"Look," Angie said. "That's where the Boston Tea Party took place."

Not the Tea Party again, thought Shelby. She didn't think an analysis of the Revolutionary War was the conversation that was going to set romantic sparks flying.

That's when Angie went to take a drink of her soda and spilled it all over the table.

"Look," Scott said and pointed at the spilled drink. "That's where the Boston soda party took place."

Everyone laughed, but Angie's laughter was nervous. Nonito grabbed a handful of napkins and helped her clean it up. Shelby came to the rescue and directed the conversation to a more user-friendly topic—the Red Sox. She pulled out the article on Ricky Baines and read some of the highlights. The guys all instantly weighed in with their opinions.

All three were Red Sox fans, although Jerry more than the others. All three thought Baines was being silly, although Nonito suggested that maybe someone else might be causing all the bad luck.

Angie was convinced that it was the "Curse of the Bambino." Red Sox fans everywhere think bad luck follows the team because Sox owner Harry Frazee sold Babe "the Bambino" Ruth to the Yankees in 1920 to finance the Broadway show *No, No Nannette*. Since then Boston had never won a World Series.

"I agree with Nonito," said Shelby. "I don't think it's a coincidence. I think someone's doing this to him deliberately."

They sat and chatted for another half hour before going their separate ways. For all Shelby and Angie knew, it could have been any of them. But at least they had it narrowed down. Maybe.

Shelby went home and crashed on her bed for a couple of hours. When she woke up, she tried to figure out who had sent Angie the notes, but she kept thinking about Ricky Baines instead.

She didn't believe in coincidence. But she didn't have any idea why someone would do all that to Ricky Baines. She'd need to learn more about him.

She called Vince and Angie and asked them if they wanted to go back to Fenway Park for some follow-up investigating. That night, when Ricky took the field with his teammates, Shelby, Vince, and Angie were back in the stands.

It was obvious that most of the fans had either read or heard about what had happened to their missing outfielder. They jeered him mercilessly. Some taunted him with posters of black cats. But Ricky was undaunted. He played great, and soon the fans were excited and cheering for him again.

He got two hits and made a spectacular catch. He was breaking out of his slump. Shelby began to think his problems might all be over. She forgot about the mystery and started cheering along with everybody else.

In the seventh inning, though, the happy mood came to a screeching halt. Ricky was chasing a line drive toward the Green Monster when something distracted him. He lost his concentration and slammed hard into the wall, where he crumpled to the ground.

Shelby and the others looked on nervously. She strained to get a clear view. When she did, she saw that Ricky Baines wasn't moving.

Chapter
4

The stadium was nearly silent as Ricky Baines lay motionless. The other outfielders were the first to reach him. The team doctor and more players were close behind. After a few moments, Ricky started to stir. First it was a shake of his leg. Then he rubbed his forehead. Finally he sat upright.

The crowd showed its relief with a roar of applause. It grew louder as Ricky got to his feet. He made a wobbly walk across the field to the Red Sox dugout. The applause grew louder with each step. It was so loud when he left the field that he raised his cap as a sign of appreciation.

"Do you think he'll be okay?" Shelby asked.

"It's a good sign that he was able to walk off on his own," Vince said.

Shelby couldn't believe the crowd. A few innings earlier, the fans had been booing him. Now he was their hero. Her heart went out to him. She wished there was some way she could help.

She started thinking about the things that had happened, looking for any possible explanations. Ricky's favorite lucky hat had disappeared while the team had been traveling. If it had been stolen, it had to have been stolen by someone who'd been traveling with the team. Moreover, she didn't know how, but she figured that it would be possible to weaken a bat so that it would splinter. But there was also the mirror, and now this accident.

It seemed impossible for one person to orchestrate all of the events. It also seemed unlikely. Who would benefit? Why would someone go to all the trouble?

The Red Sox won the game in extra innings. Once again Tom Van Ness played a key role, scoring the tying run and making an amazing catch in the tenth inning.

This night they sat in right field. After the game, Angie led them to section 42, row 37, seat 21. The seat was painted red to signify the length of the longest home run ever hit at Fenway Park. It was hit by Ted Williams and had traveled 502 feet. According to legend, it crashed through the straw hat of the man sitting in the seat. Angie pulled out her camera and had Shelby take a picture of her sitting in the seat.

"If you want," Vince said, "I can show you the seat my cousin Cecil threw up on when he ate three foot-long hot dogs. It's right over there in section thirty-six." Vince thought for a moment. "Thirty-six is also how many inches of hot dog he ate. Strange." Shelby and Angie shared a look, but said nothing.

They walked down to the seats that hung over the bullpen where the Red Sox pitchers warmed up during games. One fan was hanging over the railing and calling out to unseen players. He wore an authentic-looking Red Sox jersey with the name Pesky on the back. He held out a baseball and desperately pleaded for someone to come sign it.

At first, Shelby felt bad for him. She assumed

he was trying to get the signature for a son or daughter. Then Angie pointed to the bag of balls at his feet.

"He sells them," she said with a sneer. "You can always tell by the bag they carry. They beg and plead for the autograph, get it for free, and then charge some kid for it."

"This is something I just don't get," Shelby said. "Why would anyone buy someone else's signature? It baffles me. There's no meaning to it. I can understand that if you caught a home run ball, you would want to get it signed by the guy who hit it. At least, there's some sort of connection."

"I can even understand why you might ask for an autograph if you met a ballplayer in the street," said Angie, "but paying money for one at a store—it doesn't make any sense."

They turned to Vince for agreement but instead got a guilty look. "All right," he said sheepishly. "I did it once. But it was a ball autographed by Carl Yastrzemski. It was a present for my dad."

"Well, a present's different," said Shelby.

"Much," added Angie.

Just then Pesky noticed a clump of people around a player down by the dugout. He quickly grabbed his bag of balls and rushed over there as if it were a matter of life or death.

"And you think *I* take this game too seriously," Angie joked.

As was often the case when she worked on a mystery, Shelby was lost in thought as they walked to the exit. Vince asked her how she thought Ricky's accident fit into her theory of no coincidence or luck.

"After all, it would have been impossible for someone else to cause him to hit the wall," he said.

"True. But I still don't believe in coincidence."

"I'm surprised she doesn't want to check the outfield for clues," Angie joked to Vince.

Shelby stopped cold in her tracks. "Of course."

"I was joking," Angie implored.

Shelby quickly scanned the underside of the stadium. She was looking for any way to get to the outfield.

"If only we could get into one of those hallways," she said, looking at a pair of Employee Only doorways next to a concession stand.

"Oops. Too bad. We can't," Vince said hopefully.

"You're right. They'd notice kids," Shelby said.

Angie let out a sigh of relief.

"We'll have to become employees." And with that, Shelby was off.

She noticed a long line of vendors who sold sodas in the stadium. They were piling up all their drink racks.

Vince and Angie momentarily lost sight of her as she slipped into the middle of the group. When she came back into view, she was carrying three of the racks. She even had three of the little hats the vendors wore.

"We could fight it," Angie said. "But in the end, you know she'll talk us into it."

Vince knew Angie was right. "Let's go and get it over with."

The racks made it hard to move around, but they did the trick. The three slipped past the only slightly suspicious stare of a security guard. Additions and renovations over the decades had turned the hallway into a maze of twists and turns. "Where are we going?" Vince asked.

"I don't know," said Shelby. "But I want to get a look at the outfield. I want to see if anyone could have caused that accident."

They paused when they reached a door. There was no telling if anyone might be on the other side. Shelby took a deep breath and pushed. No one was there.

The room was long and narrow—the cement walls covered with graffiti. Giant pylons rose up from one side supporting the stadium.

"Dead end," said Shelby.

"No, it's not," said Angie breathlessly. "We're inside the Green Monster!" She was barely able to contain her excitement. "I've seen it on television before."

Angie was right. They were inside the left-field scoreboard. It was one of the last manually operated scoreboards in sports. Angie explained that two or three people worked the entire game inside the wall, updating the scores of games from around the majors.

Shelby looked out one of the slats that the scorers used to watch the game. She had a perfect view of the outfield.

"I heard that some of the guys talk to the outfielders during the boring parts of the games," Vince said.

The graffiti on the wall celebrated decades of

baseball history. It had long been a tradition for visiting players to come into the scoreboard and sign their names. There were also sections that commemorated famous events that had taken place at Fenway.

"Look," Angie said, pointing to one inscription. "This is from the night Roger Clemens set the major league record with twenty strikeouts in a game."

"Here's Ted Williams's autograph," added Vince.

Angie and Vince were in heaven. Like all kids in the area, they'd been raised with stories about the Red Sox. But how many ever got inside the Monster?

Shelby, though, was new to town. The names didn't really mean much to her. She was concentrating on the mystery. She wanted to know if there was any way that someone could have caused Ricky to crash into that wall.

She looked out another one of the slats, but didn't see anything out of the ordinary. She started looking around the room. Aside from the stacks of numbers that were put up on the scoreboard, there wasn't much else in there. There was a television on a small table next to a mini-refrigerator. There was also a boom box pushed up against the wall. Shelby thought it was odd. Unlike the TV and fridge, the boom box was positioned out of the way. "I wonder what that's for?" Shelby asked as she knelt down to look at it.

"It's probably so they can listen to the game," Vince reasoned.

"No. I'm pretty sure they'd watch the game on the television." Shelby had seen stereos like it in the store. They were expensive. Certainly too expensive to leave out like this.

Vince came over to take a look, too. The speakers were detached. Oddly, they were pointed away from the room and toward the field. He flipped on the radio. They could barely hear it. "Strange," he said.

"What's this?" Shelby asked. Someone had written Lucky 7 on top of the right speaker.

Before the others could offer any opinions, the room went dark. At first Shelby thought it was Angie playing a prank. Then she realized that the stadium was being shut down for the night.

They were trapped inside the Green Monster.

Chapter
5

The room was completely dark except for a sliver of moonlight that came in through one of the slats in the scoreboard. Shelby couldn't even see her hand.

"What now?" asked Vince.

His voice startled both Shelby and Angie.

"I'm not sure," said Shelby. "Do you think we can find our way back through the hallways?"

"We got lost finding our way here," said Angie. "And that was with the lights on."

Things seemed pretty bleak.

Then it got worse.

At first the clicking was faint. But when they quieted down, they could tell for certain that someone was approaching. They stumbled around in the dark, trying to find some place to hide.

Angie hid under a table and bumped her head in the process. Vince started to climb into a garbage can before it dawned on him that he could hide *behind* it. Shelby wasn't sure what she was hiding behind. She just hoped it was big enough.

The door opened, and a flashlight beam cut across the room. Shelby tried to get a look at the person's face, but the light was too blinding. It was probably a security guard making his rounds.

Angie thought about jumping out into the open. That way, at least, they'd be shown the way out. But she wasn't sure if hiding in the Green Monster was a you-kids-should-behave kind of offense or a you-kids-are-going-to-jail one. So she kept still.

They were all relieved when the man turned around and headed back out the door. That is, they were relieved until they heard him lock it.

"Well," said Vince, "I guess we don't have to worry about finding our way through those hallways."

"Or making my curfew," added Angie. Then she had an idea. "Is anyone close to that refrigerator?"

Shelby couldn't believe it. "You're hungry?"

"No. I just want one of you to open the door."

It was right next to Vince. He opened it up, and the refrigerator light illuminated the room.

"Okay," Shelby said, "I'd call that brilliant."

"Soda," a thirsty Vince said excitedly. He grabbed a can out of the refrigerator and popped the top. He also dug into his pocket and pulled out three quarters, which he placed where the soda had been.

That, Shelby thought to herself, *is what makes Vince Vince.*

"There's a door to the outfield," Angie said. "It should be at the far end of the room." With the room semi-lit, they were able to find the narrow doorway at the edge of the scoreboard.

They quietly exited onto the outfield. For Angie it was a near-religious experience. She slipped off her sandals and felt the cold bluegrass against her bare feet.

"This is it!" she said. "I am actually standing in left field at Fenway Park."

"Stay there any longer," Vince added, "and you'll actually be arrested in left field in Fenway Park."

"Totally worth it," Angie replied. She remembered her camera. "Take a picture of me, Vince."

Vince didn't know which was stupider—the fact that she wanted a picture that could be used as evidence of her breaking the law or the fact that he was willing to take it. "Move over so I can get more of the scoreboard in it."

Shelby walked over to the approximate area where Ricky had hit the wall. Nothing seemed unusual. There was no hole in the ground or bump in the grass. In fact, everything was perfect. Shelby wondered how they kept the grass in such good shape.

Vince reminded them that there were bound to be more security guards.

"We'd better get to the dugout," Angie said. "There should be an exit over there."

The three of them ran across the field like outfielders chasing a line drive. Only they kept going until they were out of sight.

Angie wasn't sure how much of this she should recap for her father when he asked about the game. The die-hard Red Sox part of her wanted to tell him everything: the scoreboard, left field, the dugout. The more rational part, however, wanted to keep from being put on life-time probation.

The Red Sox part overtook her again when she got in the dugout. She instantly started searching for a souvenir—proof of her adventure that she could show to her unbelieving grandchildren years from then.

Shelby and Vince were more concerned with getting out. Stairs from the dugout connected to a hallway that led to the Red Sox clubhouse and then out to the street. It would only take fifteen seconds to cover the ground.

The only problem was that a woman was pacing back and forth between them and their escape.

She was obviously troubled. Even in her current state of panic, Shelby was concerned for her. Shelby was also frustrated that this woman was blocking their way.

The three of them scrunched down behind the giant bat rack and waited for her to leave. Shelby thought about Ricky's shattered bat. She took a close look at one. They seemed just like the ones that she used playing softball in P.E. class.

Angie tried to get comfortable, but she was sitting on something hard. She reached down and pulled it out. It was a baseball. An actual game ball. She smiled wide and slipped it into the pocket on her sweatshirt. Shelby gave her a stern look, but Angie wasn't about to put it back.

"Vince," Angie whispered. "Leave a couple more quarters."

The woman stopped pacing when the clubhouse door started to open. She looked expectantly at the exiting player. It was Ricky Baines. He had stayed late so that the team doctors could fully examine him. The second he saw the woman, he clenched his teeth.

"What are you doing here?" he asked.

"I wanted to see how you were doing," she said.

"Just fine," Ricky said curtly. "No thanks to you."

Tom Van Ness came out of the clubhouse, too. He smiled at the woman and said, "Hey. How ya doing?"

She just nodded back and tried to force a smile.

Tom turned to Ricky. "Come on," he said.

"Let me give you a ride home. You shouldn't drive after taking that shot to the head."

The two ballplayers left the woman even more upset than before. She gave them a moment to get to the car, and then she left.

The coast was clear. The kids ran down the hall as fast as they could. They slipped out to the street and headed home.

"Did you guys notice anything unusual?" Shelby asked as they walked to the car.

"You mean like how small the dugout is up close?" answered Vince.

"Yeah," said Angie. "I thought it'd be much bigger."

"No," said Shelby. "I meant Ricky. There was something about his eyes."

"Oh, they're dreamy," said Angie.

"No." Shelby was getting frustrated. "The way he looked at that woman. Something is going on there. I think she's a suspect."

"A suspect?" asked Vince. "But you have no idea who she is."

"Right," answered Shelby.

"And you don't really know if there's a mystery," added Angie.

"Right," said Shelby.

Vince shook his head. "Well, with that much evidence, I say, 'Lock her up!' "

As she lay in bed, Shelby thought about her no-name suspect in an unsure case. Despite Angie and Vince's joking, she thought it was coming along well.

At seven her alarm clock rattled her awake. This had not been a very good weekend for sleep. But, after back-to-back nights at Fenway Park and a day spent at the Computer Museum, there was quite a pile of things for Shelby to do around the bed-and-breakfast.

"Why are you up so early?" Shelby's grandfather asked when he saw her in the kitchen.

"I've got to get my chores done early," she explained. "I've got a fitting with Ms. Howard this afternoon."

Mike Woo smiled big. "Of course. The mysterious Spring Fling dress. When will it be done?"

"It better be soon," Shelby said. "The dance is a week from Friday."

"You'd better tell Vince to get here on Thursday," Mike said. "I've got to take enough pictures of you two to send to all our relatives in China."

Shelby rolled her eyes. "Can't we just take one and get a lot of reprints?"

"I'm not sending photos," Mike said with a smile. "I'm sending photo albums."

With that, he laughed and went back to the dining room to serve the guests, and she started washing the windows.

By Shelby's official count, there were forty-two windows at the bed-and-breakfast that needed weekly inside-and-out cleanings. (In truth, there were only forty windows, but Shelby thought two really big ones should each count double.)

Even with the early start Shelby had to rush over to meet Ms. Howard on time. Alicia Kent Howard taught costume design in the drama department at Grayson College, the same school where Shelby's grandfather taught criminology. She was an incredible seamstress, and she was helping Shelby pull off a memorable Spring Fling dress at a reasonable price. Shelby had searched nearly twenty vintage clothing stores until she'd found the right dress. It was deep blue with short sleeves and a pleated skirt. It was also made for someone about seven inches taller than Shelby.

Ms. Howard, however, had taken care of that: Shelby tried it on, and it fit perfectly. It looked better than Shelby had dreamed possible.

"Every girl at your school will be green with envy," Ms. Howard said with a smile.

"I don't care what the girls think," Shelby said.

Alicia Kent Howard let out a hearty laugh. "Don't worry, darling. He'll think it's beautiful."

Confession time. I feel totally lousy about cutting Angie out of the whole dress thing. I mean, normally she would have gone with me to all the vintage stores to look for it. But she doesn't have a date for Spring Fling. I didn't want her to feel left out, so I just didn't tell her about it on the days that I went. Now, I feel like I've made her feel even more left out. It's one of those things where you feel like no matter what you decide, you're wrong.

A few days into the secret admirer dilemma, Angie was a wreck. Every time she opened her locker, she wondered if there would be something in it. When nothing was, she got discouraged.

As they made their way through the lunch line, Shelby told her the guy was probably trying to hang back a little. "I bet he doesn't want to seem too pushy," she reasoned. "After all, he's already sent you two notes."

Angie noticed that Scott was a couple of people behind her in line. She smiled at him, but he didn't really respond. He just adjusted his glasses and looked down at his tray.

Shelby and Angie went out to their favorite bench on the patio next to the cafeteria. Vince was waiting for them.

"Why weren't you in the lunch line?" Shelby asked. She noticed he hadn't brought a lunch.

"Are you kidding?" Vince said. "Don't you remember that smell the other day? Once I got a whiff of that, I swore off the cafeteria indefinitely."

Shelby and Angie exchanged looks.

"Anyway," Vince continued, "I went to the library to check on today's edition of the *Beacon*." He held up a photocopy of the newspaper. "I want to show you something."

"What's that?" Angie asked.

"The latest article on Ricky Baines," Vince answered. "It's about him running into the wall."

In the article, unidentified teammates reported that during the fateful play Baines was distracted because he thought he heard voices in the outfield. Shelby instantly thought of the speakers they had seen inside the scoreboard. "The boom box," she said.

"To make matters worse," Vince continued, "the manager has decided to replace Baines with Van Ness in the lineup. There's even talk that the team might think of trading Ricky."

Angie couldn't believe it. "He's a local boy from Roxbury who grew up dreaming about playing for the Sox, and they're thinking of trading him?"

Angie suggested that all of this sure was handy for Tom Van Ness. "After all, he's the one benefiting from Ricky's misfortune."

Shelby agreed. "We've got to consider him a suspect."

"He's not the only one," said Vince. "This article was written by Ruth Williams."

Shelby remembered the name from the article she had first seen at the museum.

"Take a look at the picture next to her byline." Vince handed the paper to Shelby and Angie. They recognized the face in an instant. Ruth Williams was the woman they had seen pacing and waiting outside the clubhouse for Ricky Baines.

Shelby smiled.

Chapter
6

"Appointment?" Shelby's nose crinkled at the suggestion.

"Yes, you need an appointment to speak with a reporter," said the security guard, who had no visible neck and biceps as big as cantaloupes. Shelby could tell that he took his job at the *Boston Beacon* seriously. He was not about to let two kids inside the newspaper offices just because they asked nicely.

"What we have to ask her will just take a second," Angie pleaded.

"No," he corrected. "It will just take an appointment."

End of discussion.

Shelby noticed that his name tag said Ivan Hackendrup. She wondered if Hackendrup was Russian for "He who hates teenagers."

They smiled sheepishly and walked back across the lobby. If they wanted to speak to Ruth Williams, they'd need to come up with an alternative plan.

Ivan kept a suspicious eye on them as they plotted another approach to get through the main entrance to the news and feature offices.

"Whatever happened to freedom of the press?" Shelby asked indignantly.

"I think that only has to do with what they write," Angie explained.

Shelby wasn't giving up. "I think it should mean that the press is free for 'we the people' to talk to."

Shelby was desperate. Ruth Williams was their only real suspect. They'd read her articles. More importantly, they had seen her brief exchange with Baines. She was benefiting from his problems, and he was not happy about it. The problem was that the only place they could see her was at her office, which was guarded by Ivan the Terrible.

Shelby ran through all the scams that she'd ever used to elude a guard. Normally she would pose as a delivery girl or pretend to be a long-lost relative, but Ivan would remember her face. She knew that for sure. They'd have to be more creative.

"What do you say one of us faints and when he goes for help, the other just runs in through the door?"

Angie didn't respond.

"Yeah," Shelby continued, "he probably wouldn't go for help. He'd just let us lie there un-conscious."

Shelby expected a laugh, but again Angie said nothing. Shelby turned to see that her friend was no longer standing next to her. "Angie? Angie?" Shelby caught sight of her talking to a woman at the employment desk.

"Shelby," Angie said with a smile when the woman finished answering her question, "this nice woman says we have to take our applications to the human resources office." Angie nodded to a second entrance. "It's down this hall."

"Great." Shelby was truly impressed with Angie's brainstorm. Fully aware that Ivan was still watching, they waited until someone came up to ask him a question. While he was distracted, they slipped into the second entrance that led to the human resources office. They were inside the building. Now all they had to do was find Ruth Williams.

The walls of the *Boston Beacon* were decorated with framed copies of the newspaper's most historic headlines. "Titanic Strikes Iceberg." "D-Day Forces Land in Normandy." "Armstrong Walks on Moon." These helped the staff remember the lasting importance of journalism. They also helped Shelby and Angie realize how incredibly lost they were.

"That's the third time we've passed the *Titanic*," Angie said. It was impossible for them to get their bearings in the labyrinth of offices, cubicles, and desks. And it was impossible for them to ask directions. They weren't supposed to be there. They just had to keep walking as if they knew where they were going and hope to run into Ruth Williams in the process.

They might have been at it all day, but a maintenance man came to their rescue. "Can I help you?'' he asked as they almost bumped into him for the second time.

"We're looking for the sports department," Angie said.

"We're new interns," Shelby added lamely.

He smiled, knowing full well that all the interns wore name tags. "Go straight this way and turn left at the empty frame," he said. He pointed down the hall to the one frame that held no historic front page.

Shelby had wondered about it when they passed it. In fact, she wondered about it each time they had passed it. "Why is that frame empty?" she asked.

A big smile came across his face. "That one's for the Red Sox when they win the World Series," he said. "It's been empty for over eighty years." He laughed and went back to work. Shelby began to realize that this Red Sox thing ran pretty deep throughout Boston.

They finally reached the area that was home to the paper's sportswriters. Officially called the Sports Desk, it was known around the *Beacon* as the Bullpen. The walls and desks were covered with pictures of famous Boston athletes and sports memorabilia. All the desks were sloppy except for one. Sitting at that desk was Ruth Williams.

She was talking on the phone when they arrived. Shelby and Angie caught her eye, and she motioned them to sit down. Shelby instantly noticed that Ruth looked much younger than she did in the picture next to her byline. She wondered if that was intentional. Maybe people trusted information more when it came from someone who looked older.

"I need research on any unusual superstitions Red Sox players have had in the past," Ruth said into the telephone. "And I need a photographer to go down to Roxbury and get a picture of the house where Baines's mother lives."

It was obvious that she was working on another story about Ricky Baines. As she talked, Williams checked items off a list sitting in front of her. The list was on top of one of several neatly arranged stacks of paper on her desk.

Shelby tried to sneak a peek at the list. She did so by glancing down as she looked at two framed photographs sitting next to Ruth's phone.

"It's the University of Massachusetts women's

soccer team." Shelby looked up to see that Ruth had finished her phone call. Williams was talking about one of the pictures. "We made it to the national semifinals that year."

"You were on the team?" Shelby was impressed.

"Backup goalie," Ruth answered. "Just my luck, our starter was so good she went on to win a gold medal in the Olympics. I hardly ever got a chance to play." She smiled warmly. "How can I help you two?"

"We're doing a project for school," Angie said. "We're supposed to interview someone with an interesting career."

"Yes," said Shelby. "We're writing a report on it and everything." They had decided on the report approach so they could have a way to ask her questions about Ricky Baines and all his problems.

"You want to interview me?" Ruth couldn't help but be a little flattered. "What I do is not really all that interesting."

"Of course it is," said Angie. "Both of us have often talked about our desire to one day become sportswriters."

Don't push it, thought Shelby.

"Let me tell you, sportswriting is not an easy career for women," Ruth warned.

"Which is exactly the type of thing we want to find out from you," said Shelby.

"Okay," said Ruth. "I've got a little time to talk. Where are your pads?"

"Pads?" Shelby's nose crinkled again.

"Notepads. To write down the questions and answers."

Shelby couldn't believe it. How could she have forgotten to bring something to write on? "The guard took them," she said. "I don't think he likes kids."

"Are you kidding?" said Ruth. "Ivan loves kids. He's got three of his own."

Ruth opened her drawer. She pulled out two official *Boston Beacon* reporter's pads and handed them to Shelby and Angie.

"First rule of sportswriting," she said with a joking but direct tone. "Never forget your notepad."

Shelby and Angie each wrote that down. "Can you tell us how you got started?" Angie asked.

"Well, I've always loved sports. I went to college on a soccer scholarship and majored in journalism. I thought, why not combine the two?"

"What are the keys to being a good reporter?" Shelby asked.

"Do your homework, meet your deadlines, and try not to worry what other people think. Of course, it helps to break a big story every now and then."

"Like the stories about Ricky Baines and his bad luck," Shelby said, happy to get to the subject of Ricky.

Ruth smiled. "You've been following that."

"Sure," said Angie. "It must be hard to write things about people that might upset them."

This was a sensitive issue with Ruth. For the first time in the conversation, the smile left her face. "Unfortunately, it's part of the business."

They continued to talk for a while and got along well. Ruth had a lot of funny stories, and they all laughed a lot. Unfortunately, they didn't make a lot of headway on their investigation.

Shelby wanted to get a good look at the list and file on her desk, but she couldn't figure out how. Finally, it was time to wrap up the interview.

"Any last tips for aspiring female reporters?" Angie asked.

"You've got to know the game better than the male writers just to be taken seriously," answered Ruth.

"No problem," Angie said, only half-joking. "I know more about the Red Sox than anyone—except maybe my father."

This caught Ruth's interest. "Is that so?" she asked with a hint of challenge. "Maybe we should give you a little test?" Shelby hoped that Angie could back up her big talk.

"How may Sox players have won the Triple Crown?"

Angie scoffed. "That's easy. Two. Ted Williams and Carl Yastrzemski. But Teddy won it twice."

Shelby was shocked. She didn't even know what the Triple Crown was. Ruth was impressed, too. She pressed on. "Who's the only player in baseball history to win the MVP and Rookie of the Year in the same season?"

Angie didn't hesitate. "Fred Lynn."

"One more," said Ruth. "Greatest moment in Red Sox history."

Angie smirked. "Easy. Carlton Fisk putting one over the Green Monster in game six of the '75 World Series. By the way, it's the greatest moment in *baseball* history."

Ruth smiled and gave a polite round of applause. "You really do know your stuff." Ruth had an idea. "When is your assignment due?"

"Assignment?" said Angie, who by now had forgotten that they were supposedly writing a report on Ruth.

"Next week," Shelby quickly chimed in. "Why?"

"I was just wondering if it would help any for you two to cover a game with me."

"You mean like—in person?" Angie asked.

"I guess you could watch on television," Ruth kidded, "but don't you think it would be more fun to go down on the field and hang out in the press box?"

Ruth had finally stumped Angie. She couldn't even speak, she was so excited.

"It would help a lot," Shelby said.

"Let me go talk to my editor," said Ruth. She got up from her desk. "Wait here a second."

Ruth left the Bullpen and went into her editor's office. Angie was more than excited. "I can't believe we are going down on the field, in the press box, everywhere. We'll even be there when she interviews actual players."

Shelby was excited, too. But she was excited because she had a chance to check out the list and file. "Keep a lookout for me." She slipped around to the other side of the desk and started scouring it for clues. Not wanting the other reporters to be suspicious, Shelby "accidentally" knocked one of Ruth's neat piles over. That way she could straighten up and read in the process.

Angie was not happy about this. "If you mess this up for me, Shelby, I'll never forgive you."

The list was right there on the top. It was a list of all of Ricky's superstitions. Dates were written next to some of them. For example, "May 13" was written next to "broken mirror."

Shelby realized that the dates corresponded to the times the events had happened. "Is she keeping track?" asked Shelby. "Or is she planning?"

Angie didn't have a chance to answer.

"What are you doing?" asked the voice.

Ruth Williams had caught them red-handed.

Chapter
7

Shelby had instant visions of Ivan the security guard tossing her out the door.

"She was just going to use the phone," Angie stammered.

"I wanted to call my grandfather," said Shelby, "to make sure it was all right to go to the game tomorrow."

Since Ruth had no reason to doubt them, she accepted the excuse at face value. "It better be all right," she kidded. "Because my editor gave the okay. You guys can meet me at the press entrance on Yawkey Way at five o'clock sharp."

Angie was in heaven. Normally when she went along with one of Shelby's schemes she ended up trapped in a Dumpster or covered in sludge. This time, though, she was going to do something fun—incredibly fun. She was practically speechless. "Wow," she said. "This is so great."

"All I need is a note from your teacher," Ruth added in passing.

"A what?" Shelby asked.

"A note from your teacher," said Ruth. "Something explaining the assignment. My editor has to keep that kind of stuff for his records."

"Wow," Angie said again, this time speechless for a different reason. "This is so great."

Every school has at least one cool teacher. At Wilton Patriot, it was Fred Allen. Mr. Allen had taught English and humanities at the school since, in his words, "the Pilgrims went here." His past students included the mayor, half the teachers in school, and Angie's dad. He insisted students call him Fred, and signed their yearbooks in Old English. And, whenever he showed the movie *MacBeth*, he ran the projector backward during the beheading scene. That way MacBeth's head flew through the air and attached to his body. Shelby and Angie knew

11

that if they had to ask a teacher for something strange, Fred Allen was their best bet.

"Don't you see, Mr. Allen?" Angie pleaded. "I need this kind of extra credit to make up for my test the other day."

Mr. Allen looked at her curiously. "But you don't need it." He dug through a pile of freshly graded tests on his desk. "Look, here it is. You got an A on the test."

"I did?" replied a sheepish Angie.

"Yes. And you gave the best definition of *moira* that I've read in years."

I knew it, thought Shelby. *Little Miss I-Bombed-the-Test aced it.* She tried to give Angie the evil eye, but her friend avoided looking at her.

"But Shelby's grade could stand a little boost," he continued. He sorted through the tests until her giant C was on top.

Typical, thought Shelby.

He opened his grade book and ran his finger down to Shelby's name. "Your average is right on the bubble. This might be just what you need to bump it up a grade."

"To an A?" Shelby asked hopefully.

"To a B minus," answered Mr. Allen. Then,

sensing Shelby's disappointment, he added, "a strong B minus."

This is so my life, thought Shelby. *I'm about to do somersaults of joy for a strong B- and Angie's upset about her A.* Shelby rationalized it in her head. *I bet Dr. Watson made better grades than Sherlock Holmes.*

Mr. Allen started to write out a letter for Ruth Williams and her editor. Shelby was thrilled because she would be able to get close up to the mystery. Angie was thrilled because she would be able to get close up to the Red Sox. Everyone was thrilled.

Then Mr. Allen looked up from the letter.

"Do you think seven hundred words will be enough?" he said with a kindly smile.

"Enough for what?" asked Shelby.

"For your extra-credit essay," answered the teacher. "You did plan on writing an essay, didn't you?"

Shelby had kind of hoped she'd pick up the points just for showing up.

"Of course." Angie did her best to force a smile.

"Seven hundred words should be plenty," continued Shelby.

Shelby and Angie walked through the halls with the weight of a seven-hundred-word essay hanging over them.

"Just what you want when you're heading into finals," Angie said. "A nice gigantic essay."

"Seven hundred words," Shelby said. "That's a lot." She started working on an opening sentence. "For a woman, being a sportswriter is very, very difficult." Shelby counted the words on her fingers as she spoke. "That's just ten," she said and instantly became worried.

She started again. "For a woman, being a sportswriter is very, very, very, very difficult."

"I don't think you can just add six hundred and ninety more *verys*," Angie replied. "Fred would probably catch on."

Up ahead they saw Vince trying to look discreet while watching Angie's locker. The three of them had been taking turns keeping an eye on the locker between classes. The idea was that one of them would catch the secret admirer in the act. But so far, Operation Stakeout was turning out more like Operation Strikeout.

"No sign of him," said Vince.

"Maybe he lost interest," said Angie. She was

beginning to think she might never find out who sent the notes.

Shelby rolled her eyes. "Would you stop being so negative?"

The three of them walked together to Angie's locker. Shelby informed Vince of her homework assignment. He couldn't help but laugh. He was jealous that they were going to get behind the scenes at the game. The assignment took the sting out of it a little bit.

Inside Angie's locker, there were two long-stemmed red roses. They were beautiful. A note was attached to them.

"How did those get in there?" a stunned Vince asked.

"Good question," said Shelby. "I know you don't have much experience with stakeouts, but you should have noticed a guy carrying flowers."

"There is no way he came and did that while I was watching. No way."

Shelby and Vince went back and forth at each other for a little bit, while Angie just silently read the note.

"Well?" asked Shelby. "What does it say?"

Angie played coy for a moment. Then a big smile came over her face. She read it out loud.

"Roses blossom
Every spring.
We'd be awesome
At the Fling.

"Then down here he wrote, 'I hope you don't have a date yet.' "

"Do you?" asked Vince, apparently unaware that such information probably would have been discussed by now.

Guys are so clueless, thought Shelby.

"Yeah," said Angie. "I'm going with Tom Cruise. But I need a backup in case Nicole Kidman gets jealous."

"How come she gets to be sarcastic and I don't?" asked Vince.

"That's just the way it is," Shelby said matter-of-factly. She was excited for Angie, but she was also intrigued. "Even if we forget that old eagle eyes over here missed him, I can't figure out how he got the roses into the locker."

"What do you mean?" asked Angie.

"Well, a note's one thing," said Shelby. "All you've got to do is slide it through the slats. But roses? You'd have to open the door. Which means you'd have to get past the lock."

"Whatever," Angie said as she admired her roses. She would wait until later to worry about that. Right now she just wanted to enjoy the moment.

Angie was still smiling as they drove into Boston. They met Ruth Williams right on time at the press entrance to Fenway Park.

Ruth smiled when she saw them. "Pads?" she asked expectantly.

Shelby and Angie both smiled back and held up their notepads.

"So," Ruth said. "You've got the first lesson down."

"And a note from our teacher," Angie said, handing over Mr. Allen's letter.

Ruth scanned it quickly. "Ouch. Seven hundred words. Time to whip out the adjectives."

Shelby and Angie were happy to be with someone who understood the difficulties of teenage life. Before they went into the stadium, Ruth handed them their credentials, which were to be worn at all times in the ballpark.

"There are certain rules for anyone carrying a press credential," she said. "First, you're not allowed to ask for autographs. We're all here as working professionals."

"Easy enough," said Shelby. Angie nodded in agreement.

"Second, journalists are supposed to be neutral," she said. "That means no cheering for either team."

Angie couldn't imagine going to a Red Sox game and not cheering. "Not even if someone hits a home run?" she asked hopefully.

"Not even if someone hits a grand slam with one hand covering his eyes," Ruth responded.

"No cheering," agreed Angie.

"Okay, let's get to work," Ruth said. They flashed their credentials to the guard and walked inside. Ruth explained that the best time to work on a story was before a game.

"Baseball players are incredibly impatient," she explained. "They hate waiting around for the game to start. They'll talk to help pass the time."

Ruth told them that she had learned this the

hard way when she covered her first game. "I thought the interviewing was done after the game," she said. "I started asking all these in-depth questions and the players were all in a rush to get home. I had to fill ten column inches and I had nothing but a couple of quotes from the bat boy."

"What'd you do?" Angie asked.

"The same thing you guys are going to do with that assignment," Ruth said.

"Last night the Red Sox lost a very, very, very tough game," said Shelby.

"Exactly. The bat boy framed a copy of the article though," Ruth added. All three of them were laughing.

They walked out onto the field while the Red Sox were taking batting practice. Shelby looked at the players standing around the cage waiting their turn. It looked just like the kids in her P.E. class waiting to bat in softball.

"We're allowed to talk to the players here between the dugout and the batting cage," she said. "But you can't cross the foul line or go over by the outfield."

Angie was too speechless to have any problem

with it. She had to keep her cool and act as if she belonged down here with all her favorite players. She and Shelby stayed back so that Ruth could work a little without having them in her hair.

They saw Ruth try to talk to Ricky, but he would have nothing to do with her. He jogged to the safe haven of the outfield to practice catching fly balls. Shelby heard one of the players refer to this as "shagging" flies.

Angie pointed out everyone for Shelby. She told her all the names of the guys playing catch right in front of them. One of them noticed her interest.

"Want to play?" He motioned to a ball and glove lying nearby on the ground.

"Me?" Angie could hardly believe it.

"Sure," he said.

Angie picked up the ball and glove, and the two of them got clear of everyone else.

Don't make a fool of yourself, Angie said to herself. She wanted to make sure she threw it hard enough, so she put a little extra zing on the ball. A little too much. The player had to whip his glove in front of his face to keep from getting his nose broken. Angie smiled sheepishly.

"Maybe we should stand a little farther apart," he said as he took a half-dozen steps backward.

Ruth saw what was going on. She told the *Beacon*'s photographer to take a picture of them so that she could give it to Angie.

Shelby didn't know where to look for clues. The victim and both of her suspects were there. But nothing seemed out of the ordinary. They were just working. She was amazed at all the work that it took to put on a baseball game. The field was buzzing with activity. The groundskeepers were especially busy. Shelby still couldn't figure out how they kept the grass so nice.

She noticed one groundskeeper looking around the Red Sox dugout. Something about him seemed familiar. Then she recognized him. It was the guy who was begging for autographs over the bullpen the other night.

He noticed her looking at him. He quickly put his head down and started walking around the batting cage. Shelby noticed he was carrying something in his back pocket.

She tried to remember the name that was on the back of the Red Sox jersey he had been wearing. "Pesky," she said out loud.

Once he heard this, he started jogging down the left field foul line. He was heading straight for the Green Monster.

Shelby started to follow him. She instantly forgot about where she was and wasn't allowed to go on the field.

She almost caught up to him about twenty feet from the wall, but she was too focused on him to notice that she'd walked on to the field of play. Ricky Baines was chasing after a fly ball at that same moment. Neither Shelby nor Ricky noticed the other until it was too late.

At the last second, Shelby looked up and saw him barreling right at her.

Chapter

8

There was no way for Shelby to avoid the hard-charging Ricky. The two of them collided right along the left field foul line. Considering the fact that Ricky was six foot three and 185 pounds, Shelby got the short end of the collision stick. She felt the air rush out of her body as she crumpled to the ground. In her delirium, Shelby could only think of a balloon with its end suddenly untied.

Ricky instantly scrambled to help her. "Are you okay?"

Shelby gasped a couple of quick breaths. "I think I'm fine," she said. Her ribs were throbbing, and her ankle was sore. She thought maybe she had twisted it.

Ricky bent over her, obviously concerned. "I'm so sorry," he said as he helped her up to her feet.

"No. *I'm* sorry," Shelby said. "It was all my fault. They warned us not to go in the outfield."

Shelby was relieved to get her air back. She tested the ankle. It was tender but seemed to work okay. Suddenly she started to worry about Ruth. She didn't want to be seen in an area where she had specifically been told not to go.

"I better take you in to see the team doctor," Ricky said. "That ankle is obviously sore."

"No. Really. I'm fine." Shelby tried not to wince in pain when she stood up. "See. Just like new. You better get back out to practice."

Shelby was impressed that a big-time star would be so concerned about her. She had heard and read so many stories about athletes not caring. But this guy obviously wasn't like that. It made her want to solve the mystery that much more.

"If you're sure?" he asked.

"Positive." Shelby just smiled and moved off the playing field. "Thanks." Shelby thought back to Ricky hobbling off the other night. She couldn't help but wonder what it was like to do it with thirty-four thousand people screaming their lungs out.

By the time Shelby was back on her feet, Pesky, the fake groundskeeper, had disappeared. The only way out was through the Green Monster. She made sure there were no ballplayers coming her way, and she exited through the door.

There was so sign of Pesky or anybody else in the scoreboard. It was still over an hour before the game, and the scorers didn't have anything to do yet. Shelby went over to where she had seen the boom box the other night. It was gone.

She had several pieces of the mystery, but none of them seemed to fit together. A baseball cap is stolen in Kansas City. A man dressed like a groundskeeper is digging through the dugout and then disappears through the outfield wall. A boom box is in the scoreboard one night and gone the next.

It'll have to wait, she thought. *I've got to get back to Angie and Ruth.* Shelby was concerned that they'd wonder where she was.

"Did anyone notice me missing?" Shelby asked Angie when she returned.

"You were gone?" Angie was still riding high from playing catch on the field.

They looked over at Ruth and a group of reporters talking to Tom Van Ness.

"It's been quite a while since anyone's wanted to hear what I had to say," he joked. "What's the matter? Are all the superstars busy?" It was obvious that he was enjoying the newfound attention.

One of the reporters asked him about his success in the wake of Ricky's troubles.

"I think Ricky's a great kid with a super future," said Van Ness. "And while he's working on these problems, it's my job to do the best I can to fill in for him."

Ruth noticed a cut on his hand and asked him about it. He told them it happened when he was working on his boat down at the marina.

"Earlier in the season I believed everything you all wrote about my career coming to an end," he said. "I was down at the marina looking for a new job." He flashed a big smile, but it was obvious that he had not appreciated what had been written about him.

Before anyone could ask another question, the Red Sox manager called everybody in, signaling the end of batting practice. It was time to get off the field.

"See you guys later," Tom said with wink.

Shelby didn't know what to make of him. One thing was certain. The worse things got for Baines, the better they were for Van Ness.

Ruth approached Shelby and Angie. "So, are you two hungry?"

This was the big surprise that Ruth had been keeping from them. Like all ballparks, Fenway had a huge buffet laid out for the sportswriters working the game. It was filled with meats, side dishes, and great desserts.

"Fattening the pigs before the slaughter," Ruth said, scooping up a slice of lasagna. "Every stadium has its highlights. The ribs in Kansas City are world class."

This caught Shelby's attention. "That's when the hat was stolen," she whispered. The teenagers piled their plates high. This was no visit to the school cafeteria. By the time the game started, they were sitting in the press box behind giant mounds of food. They had not fully trusted Ruth when she said they could go back for seconds. They wanted to be sure.

93

"My dad won't believe this." Angie bit into a barbecued chicken leg. It was delicious.

Conversation in the press box was lively. The reporters worked together almost every night for seven months. During that time they developed a sense of camaraderie.

Angie liked to hear all the inside scoops and gossip. A reporter from New York told her that one of the Yankees' star players was actually afraid of the dark. "He sleeps with a little baseball-shaped night-light," the reporter told her with a wink.

Much of the press box gossip was about Ricky Baines and his "bad luck" troubles.

"He'll be traded by the end of the month," one reporter said with great certainty. "My guess is San Francisco."

"You really think they'd trade him just for this?" Angie asked.

"It's distracting," another reporter said. "Besides, Van Ness is playing so well. They need to trade him while they can still get someone good in return."

"That would be a classic Red Sox deal," Angie continued, suddenly one of the experts. She started listing all-stars that Boston had let get away. "Carlton Fisk, Brady Anderson, Jeff Bagwell, Roger Clemens. The list goes on."

"What do you know," said the reporter from New York. "A kid who actually knows a little about the game."

"Are you kidding?" Ruth said. "She knows more about the Red Sox than any of you bums."

With that, the writers started another game of "Stump Angie." One by one they tossed out Red Sox trivia questions at her. They started off easy, but soon they got hard. She was more than up to the challenge, getting almost all of them right.

She even stumped the entire group of writers with a question about the Green Monster. "Why are there dots and dashes along the edge of the scoreboard?" she asked.

Not one of them knew that the dots and dashes were Morse code for the initials of Tom and Jean Yawkey, the husband and wife who'd owned the team for decades.

While everyone was busy playing Red Sox trivia, Shelby slipped away to the rest room. She wanted to do a little snooping around.

She took a few minutes to poke around the clubhouse, hoping she might see Pesky again.

Shelby was amazed by how unexceptional everything was. With all the million-dollar salaries, she expected to find a state-of-the art athletic facility. But the tunnels down by the dugout and clubhouse were old and damp. The wood floor creaked as she walked across it. Not exactly ideal sleuthing conditions.

"Hey," a deep voice called out from behind. "What are you doing down here?"

Shelby knew she was busted. She cringed as she turned to see—Ricky Baines. His demeanor changed instantly.

"It's you," he said. "Are you hurt?"

"A little," Shelby said, figuring compassion would be a helpful thing. "My ribs are sore. And my ankle."

"Let's get you an ice pack." He motioned her toward the clubhouse.

"Don't you need to stay in the dugout?" Shelby asked.

"No. It's okay," Ricky said. "Coach isn't going to put me in tonight." Shelby could tell by his voice that he was disappointed.

Ricky led her through the empty locker room. "Don't worry," he said. "No one's in here, so you won't see anything you're not supposed to see."

Like the hallway, the clubhouse was kind of dingy. It wasn't really that much better than the locker rooms at school. She couldn't help thinking that the Red Sox could use her grandfather to do a makeover on the clubhouse area just as he had done on the bed-and-breakfast.

Ricky reached into a cooler by the trainer's table and grabbed an ice pack. Shelby looked over and saw Ricky's name inscribed above a locker. Right next to it was the locker for Tom Van Ness. She noticed suitcases sitting in the lockers.

"Going someplace?" she asked as she put the pack on her ankle.

"Straight to the airport and off to Texas to play the Rangers," Ricky said.

"I really want to apologize for getting in your way earlier," Shelby said.

"It wasn't your fault," Ricky said. "It's me and this bad luck. It's rubbing off on other people now."

He looked up to see her reaction. "I know that most people think it's all silly," he said. "But I just can't help who I am. I'm always looking for signs. Like the time. Whenever I look at a clock and see that it's eleven-eleven I know it's good luck."

"Why eleven-eleven?" Shelby asked.

"Because it's the same backward, forward, and upside-down." He could tell by Shelby's look that she was skeptical. "Did you know that World War One ended at eleven o'clock on the eleventh day of the eleventh month?"

No, I didn't, Shelby thought. She quickly filed it way as a possible question to stump Angie with later.

"Did you ever think someone might be doing all these things to you on purpose?" Shelby asked.

"Who would do it?" asked Ricky.

"Do you have any enemies?" Shelby asked.

"Just one," he answered. "And it couldn't have been him."

"Who is it?" Shelby wondered what it would take for someone to consider him an enemy.

"There's this one guy," Ricky said. "He runs

a baseball-card shop. You've got to understand, I really hate some of these guys. They rip off kids. It's bad. Anyway, my brother went into his store and saw that he was selling baseballs autographed by me. Only, my brother could tell it wasn't my signature. He told me about it and I told the police."

Shelby instantly thought of the fake grounds-keeper. "Was his name Pesky?" she asked.

"No. It was Jenkins," Ricky said. "His store is in the North End on Prince Street."

Shelby made a mental note of this.

She looked around the locker room, hoping to see the boom box. They heard some cheering outside.

"I better get back out there," he said.

"Thanks for the ice pack."

Shelby went back up to the press box. The caterer was bringing in freshly grilled hot dogs. They smelled great. Shelby told Angie all about her two meetings with Baines. "Your cousin was right," Shelby said. "He's really nice. We've got to help him."

"We better make it quick," said Angie. "These guys are talking like he'll be traded any day now. Oh, and I found out something else," she added. "Guess who's Ricky's roommate when they travel on the road?"

Shelby thought for a moment. "Tom Van Ness," Shelby said. Angie nodded in agreement.

The only disappointing part of the evening was that the Red Sox lost the game 6–2. On the bright side, this made it easy for Angie to keep her no-cheering promise.

A group of writers was going out and asked Ruth if she wanted to come along. "No thanks," she said. "I've got to get back to the paper and finish my column."

This caught Angie's attention. She pulled Shelby aside. "She already finished her column," Angie whispered. "I saw her e-mail it in to her editor."

Shelby couldn't figure this one out. "We'll talk about it in the car," she whispered back.

They thanked Ruth for such a wonderful evening. "My pleasure," she told them. "Oh, I had the photographer take pictures of both of you. I should have them back by Thursday or Friday. Give me a call and I'll give you some prints."

They thanked her again and promised her they'd send her a copy of their essay.

They felt bad for doing it, but they followed Ruth when she left the stadium. As they suspected, she didn't go to the newspaper offices. Instead, she took a roundabout way to a posh suburb.

She pulled up in front of a very nice house. Looking both ways to make sure no one had seen her, she unlocked the front door and went inside.

"That's a pretty fancy house for a young reporter," Angie said.

Shelby had to agree. "Maybe it's her parents' house."

Angie motioned to the mailbox that stood at the end of the driveway. "There's only one way to find out."

Shelby cautiously made her way up to the mailbox and read the name on the side. Angie was right. The house wasn't Ruth's. It belonged to Ricky Baines.

Chapter
9

According to Ricky, the Red Sox were supposed to leave for the airport immediately after the game. That meant Ruth Williams was in his house alone.

"If Ricky's too angry to talk to her," Shelby surmised, "what do you think the odds are he wants her alone in his house?"

Suddenly the broken mirror made sense. If Ruth was able to get into his house, she could have slipped in while he was in the shower and knocked the mirror down. By the time he got out of the shower, she could have been long gone.

"We need to find out if Ruth was covering the team in Kansas City when Ricky's cap got stolen," Shelby said. "She did mention how good the ribs were there."

"But she's so nice," said Angie. "Look at all the great stuff she did for us tonight."

"I know," said Shelby. "But we just saw her sneak into his house."

Before they could talk about it any more, the front door opened. Shelby and Angie slid down low in their seats to make sure they couldn't be seen.

Ruth exited the house carrying a small box under her arm. It was too dark to get a good look at it. She put it in the trunk of her car and drove away.

They didn't want to think that Ruth was guilty, so they avoided the subject and talked about Angie's secret admirer all the way home.

"I know it's not Nonito," Angie said. "It turns out he still has a girlfriend back at his old school. She's even driving up to go to Spring Fling."

"That leaves Scott or Jerry," Shelby said.

Angie took a deep breath. "I hope it's Jerry," she said.

"Why?" asked Shelby.

"Scott's nice enough," Angie said, "but he's too much of a joker. He never takes anything seriously. Jerry and I would be more compatible. Besides, Jerry asked me if I was doing anything after we go to the Computer Museum on Saturday. I think he's going to make the dance thing official."

Shelby smiled. "That's it, then. Why were you keeping this a secret?"

"I don't know. It's so junior high. Hey, if I'm going to Spring Fling, I've got to pick out a dress," Angie said. "You, too; it's next Friday, isn't it?"

Shelby cringed. "I've already got my dress," she said. She could tell that Angie was surprised and a little hurt. "I figured you'd be bored going with me to try on clothes."

Angie could see right through her. "I wouldn't have minded," she said. "But that's not why you didn't tell me. You don't have to worry about hurting my feelings."

"It's not that," Shelby said.

"I know," said Angie. "It's just that I know you get awkward sometimes about the whole Vince-you thing. Trust me. I'm not jealous. I've accepted that a little third-wheel action is part of my life."

"Okay," said Shelby. "I'm sorry."

"Don't worry about it. Besides, I'm not going to be Dateless in Boston anymore." She smiled broadly.

"That's right," Shelby said. "You've got Jerry."

They were both happy as clams. There was only one problem. Jerry wasn't the secret admirer. It was Scott.

Vince was the one who figured it out. The next day he was getting his books out of his locker when he noticed that the back panel could wiggle loose. *That's it*, he thought. *That's how he got the roses into her locker without opening the lock. He slipped them in from the locker on the opposite side.* All Vince had to do was go to the bank of lockers that backed up to Angie's. Scott's locker was directly behind hers.

He very proudly explained this to Shelby as they drove into Little Italy after school that day. Vince was going to get his hair cut at his Uncle Fausto's barbershop.

Shelby was impressed by Vince's detective

skills, but disappointed in the result. "Angie's got her heart set on Jerry," she told him. "She might not take this well."

Vince thought about it for a moment. "Then we'll convince her that Scott's a better catch," Vince said. He parked the car right in front of Rosania's Barbershop.

"*La bella Shelby, buon giorno,*" boomed Uncle Fausto when they walked into the shop. "What are you doing here today?"

"I want to make sure Vince doesn't have another accident," Shelby said. "And don't tell me you don't know what I'm talking about." The accident in question happened the last time Vince went in for a haircut. Uncle Fausto had a rule: Vince got all his haircuts free, but he could only speak Italian in the barbershop. That way, he would keep in touch with his Italian heritage. The problem was that Vince's Italian was not so great, and he had asked that the haircut be "not too short." Unfortunately, he used the wrong words and actually said, "extremely short." When Uncle Fausto was done, Vince was practically bald. Since this was going to be the "Spring Fling haircut," Shelby wanted it to turn out perfect. After all, her grandfather was planning to send albums of pictures. She thought Vince should at least look like himself.

Vince sat down in the chair, and Uncle Fausto went to work. Opera music played in the background. Shelby just sat back and enjoyed the inevitable conversations.

"How come I don't see you around here more often?" Uncle Fausto asked. He waived the Italian-only rule when Shelby came with Vince.

"I try to, but I'm busy with school and work," Vince said.

Uncle Fausto turned to Shelby. "He's been treating you right?"

"Very nice, Mr. Rosania," said Shelby.

"Please, please, call me Uncle Fausto."

Shelby liked being included in Vince's family. Other than her grandfather, all of her relatives lived far away. Most of them were still in China.

Vince's Aunt Flavia came down from their apartment above the barbershop. She always doted on Vince. She came over and gave him a big kiss. She was carrying a plate of Italian rice balls called *suppli.* Shelby had never seen Aunt

Flavia when she wasn't carrying a plate of something.

Uncle Fausto gave Vince a terrific haircut. As always, Vince tried to pay him. As always, Uncle Fausto wouldn't hear of it. He suggested that he use the money to treat Shelby to some *gelato*, a type of Italian ice cream.

They said their goodbyes and went walking down Prince Street together, holding hands. Shelby loved the ethnic neighborhoods in Boston. As they walked through Little Italy, they could have been walking through a neighborhood in Rome. The sidewalks were filled with crates of vegetables, and the smells of fresh bread and delicious sauces filled the air. Even the music drifting out of people's windows was sung in Italian.

Sometimes Shelby would take Vince to Boston's Chinatown along Beach Street. Shelby had lived in China until she was a teenager, so her Chinese was perfect. She loved to take Vince to restaurants and get him to try different foods.

They were trying to figure out how to tell Angie about Scott when Shelby saw the sign for Beantown Ball Cards.

"I bet that's the one," she said.

Vince didn't know what she was talking about.

"Ricky Baines told me that his only enemy was a guy who ran a baseball shop on Prince street."

"Let's check it out," said Vince.

She walked into the store and saw that it was run by none other than Pesky, the fake groundskeeper.

Okay, let me say that there were plenty of opportunities for someone to point out that Pesky was the name of a famous Red Sox player. I'd been going around thinking that the guy's name was "Pesky." Instead, it turns out that his name is Bud Jenkins and he is the guy that Ricky reported for selling fake autographs.

"Act like you don't know me," she whispered to Vince. She didn't know if Pesky would recognize her from the ballpark. (Of course, it's kind of hard to forget a teenage girl who gets run over by a speeding outfielder.) Luckily, Jenkins was busy sorting through a stack of baseball cards and hadn't noticed her come in.

The store was filled with much more than just baseball cards. There were all sorts of memorabilia, ranging from autographed pictures to authentic uniforms.

"Can I help you?" Jenkins asked Vince.

"Just looking," Vince said. He noticed a row of baseball caps. "Are those real?" he asked.

"Worn in actual games," Jenkins bragged and went back to sorting cards.

Shelby slid next to Vince and pretended to look through a notebook of autographed pictures. "Find out if he has a Ricky Baines cap," she whispered.

"How much for a Ricky Baines hat?" Vince asked.

Jenkins laughed. "Those are pretty hard to come by."

"Oh," said Vince. "I had heard this was the ultimate location for getting Red Sox memorabilia." He hadn't actually heard it, but he had read it on the business card Jenkins had put out on the counter.

"It is," Jenkins said. "I didn't say it was impossible to get. I just said it was hard."

He smiled a salesman's smile.

That's when Shelby noticed the boom box on the shelf. It looked like the one they had seen inside the Green Monster. But the only way Shelby could know for sure was by looking to see if Lucky 7 was written on top of the right speaker.

While Jenkins was showing Vince the caps, Shelby tried to get closer to the boom box. It was too high on the shelf. She tried to climb up by putting her foot on a box. Vince saw what was going on and tried to keep Jenkins from looking that way.

It was pointless a few moments later, when the box gave way and Shelby tumbled into a display of game programs.

Jenkins recognized her the second he saw her. "You!" he bellowed. "What are you doing here?"

Jenkins looked pretty scary as he walked over to Shelby. She scampered to her feet and bolted for the door.

Within seconds, Vince and Shelby were running down Prince Street with Bud Jenkins hot on their trail.

"You're a lot of fun to be with," Vince said as they turned the corner.

"Just run!" Shelby answered.

They hadn't really done anything wrong. But they could tell that didn't make much difference to Jenkins.

He was gaining on them. They had gotten a head start while he was locking the door, but he was fast. A smile came over his face when he saw them turn in to an alley. He knew it was a dead end.

He stopped at the sidewalk to catch his breath. He heard a garbage can rattle on the other side of a storage shed. He jumped around the corner of the shed. "Gotcha!"

He was surprised to see the looming, unsmiling face of Fausto Rosania.

"I never realized he was so big," Shelby whispered to Vince as they watched from the back of Uncle Fausto's barbershop.

Chapter
10

Thwap! The ball rocketed off the bat in a low arc that carried it inches above the infielder's outstretched glove. It was what long-time baseball fans called a frozen rope. Shelby cheered as her classmate sprinted around first base and slid into second just ahead of the throw.

"Way to hit the ball into the gap, Carl!" she shouted from her spot in the dugout. She turned to Vince and Angie. "Did you see that? That ball was outside and he still managed to drive it to the opposite field."

Vince couldn't believe this was the same girl who had never heard of the Green Monster just a few days before. "Check out 'Shelby Ballgame' over here," he said to Angie.

"Yeah. Pretty soon she'll be spitting," Angie offered.

Shelby thought about spitting, but she couldn't bring herself to do it. There were limits. Instead, she just clapped and tried a little chatter. "Come on, batter. Big hit."

There were a half-dozen kids ahead of them in the batting order, so they had some time to kill while they waited. They started to consider suspects.

"Well, there's Ruth Williams," Shelby said. "She's been scooping everyone with her coverage of Ricky and his troubles."

"Makes you wonder if it's hard work or if it's because she's been manufacturing the story," Vince said. "After all, we all saw her have that argument with him after the game."

"And we saw her sneak into his house when he was on a road trip," Angie added.

"I just wish I knew what was in that box she was carrying," said Shelby.

Scott Bushnell came up to the plate. Shelby and Vince took the opportunity to talk him up to Angie. "Hey, here's Scott," Shelby said. "Are you sure you're not hoping he's the one?"

Scott swung at the first pitch and slugged it all of four feet.

"Yeah, I'm sure," said Angie.

The pitcher picked up the ball and tossed it to the first baseman, getting Scott out by a mile.

"You're out," yelled Coach Croom.

Scott humorously clutched his chest and collapsed on first base. Shelby and Vince both laughed a little more than was merited.

"He sure is funny," said Vince.

Shelby realized that Angie wasn't interested and went back to talking over the suspects. "There's always Bud Jenkins," Shelby said.

"It's very weird that he was sneaking around the game as a groundskeeper," Vince said. "Maybe that's how he tampered with the bat and stole the hat."

That was the weak link for Shelby. "But the hat was stolen in Kansas City," she said.

"True," Vince said. "But he said he could get the hat."

"He's also got a great motive," added Shelby. "I checked the records on the computer down at the police station. He was fined fifteen hundred dollars when Ricky turned him in for selling fake autographs."

Jerry Hubbs came up to bat next. Angie watched him closely. Shelby could tell that Angie was in full crush mode. She didn't know what to do, but she foresaw a major relationship collision coming.

"He's on the tennis team," Angie said. "Check out his extension when he swings the bat." Jerry swung the bat perfectly as he drilled the next pitch into next year. It carried well over the deepest outfielders. Jerry jogged around the bases with ease.

Vince looked over at Scott. *Poor guy*, he thought.

They got back to talking about the case. "Jenkins may have a good motive, but we're still only talking fifteen hundred dollars," Angie said. "Tom Van Ness has a two-million-dollar reason."

"Where do you get that number?" asked Vince.

"That's how much the Red Sox owe him if they extend his contract another year," Angie said. "Three weeks ago that seemed unlikely. Today, it's almost a certainty."

"Two million dollars is a lot of money," Shelby agreed. All three of the suspects benefited from Ricky's troubles. Ruth Williams got a great story, Tom Van Ness got more playing time and potentially more money, and Bud Jenkins got revenge. All three of them were also tied to decent evidence.

This case had Shelby baffled. This wasn't like most of the cases she worked on. There was no missing jewelry to uncover or burglar to catch. She wasn't even sure if an actual crime had been committed. The cap had been stolen, but its actual value was probably only about twenty dollars. It wasn't nice that someone had taken advantage of Ricky. But it had been his decision to believe in good and bad luck. No one had made him do it.

Angie picked up a bat and warmed up a little. She was up next. Shelby didn't know what to do about her and her secret admirer. She had until Saturday to convince her friend that Scott was just as good as Jerry. It seemed far enough away.

"Did I tell you about the e-mail I sent?" Angie asked.

Shelby had a sick feeling in her stomach. "To whom? When?" Shelby asked.

"To Jerry. Today. I decided to speed up the process and just tell him that I would go to Spring Fling with him."

Shelby and Vince exchanged looks as Angie walked up to the plate.

"This is going to get pretty ugly," said Vince.

Chapter
11

"How could you let this happen?" Angie moaned when Shelby told her that Scott was actually her secret admirer. "You knew who it was and you didn't tell me?"

"I just found out," Shelby said. "I was still trying to figure out how to break the news to you. Besides, I didn't know you would go off and do something as crazy as e-mail Jerry."

"That e-mail says, 'Yes, I'd love to go to Spring Fling with you.' Do you see the problem with that, Shelby? He didn't ask me." Angie couldn't believe it. "By this time tomorrow, I'll be the laughingstock of the entire school."

"Look on the bright side," Shelby said, trying to sound encouraging.

"What exactly *is* the bright side?" Angie demanded.

Shelby thought for a moment. "I'll tell you when I think of it." Shelby sat quietly for the rest of the drive to the *Boston Beacon*. Officially, they were going to pick up their photographs from the baseball game. Unofficially, though, Shelby was hoping to figure out Ruth's role in this whole business.

Ivan the Terrible recognized Shelby immediately. She had been looking forward to this mini-reunion. *Let's see you stop me this time*, Shelby said to herself as she approached the guard's desk.

"We're here to see Ruth Williams," Shelby offered with more than a hint of defiance.

"Yes, Ms. Woo, Ms. Burns, she's expecting you." He smiled and held open the door for them. *Ruth was right*, Shelby thought. *He is a nice guy.*

This time they found the sports desk with no problem—although Angie did feel a slight shock of anxiety when she passed the *Titanic* page yet another time.

"Shelby, Angie," Ruth called out when she saw them. "The pictures are over there." She motioned them to an art table that was covered with photographs.

Ruth seemed to be in a bit of a rush. In fact, there was a lot of activity around the sports desk. This seemed odd because the Red Sox had just gotten back from a road trip and weren't going to play again until the next day.

"What's all the excitement?" Angie asked.

"Press conference at Fenway," said Ruth as she picked up one of the many organized lists on her desk. "Looks like they're trading Baines to San Francisco."

"When are they making the announcement?" Shelby asked.

"In about two hours," Ruth said as she checked her watch. Shelby and Angie were stunned. They weren't going to solve the mystery in time. They quietly started digging through the pictures on the art table.

"They're really going to trade him," Shelby said. She couldn't believe it. "He's going to have to leave his family and friends."

"San Francisco's pretty far away," Angie added.

A few moments later Angie found the picture of her playing catch.

"That's a great picture," Shelby said.

"I like it," said Angie.

The photographer had snapped it just as Angie was releasing the ball. The Green Monster was right behind her in the background. The Red Sox players were standing around her. It was perfect.

"I think I'll get it framed and give it to my dad," she said. "Father's Day is next month."

They started looking for the other picture when something caught Shelby's eye. Tucked underneath Ruth's desk was the box they had seen her take out of Ricky's house the other night.

Shelby had to find out what was in it.

Ruth had stepped into her editor's office to talk about the press conference. There was a lot of commotion. Maybe no one would notice her.

Shelby kneeled down and gently nudged the box out from under the desk. She opened one flap and tried to get a good look in the box. It was filled with books and compact discs.

Do the discs have something to do with the boom box in the scoreboard? she wondered.

Then she noticed the frame and the picture of Ruth and Ricky holding hands.

"That's personal!" Shelby glanced up to see Ruth staring down at her. Her voice sounded more worried than angry. "You have no business looking in there."

There was another picture of them kissing.

"Now it makes sense," Shelby said, realizing. "Ricky's your boyfriend. That's why you went into his house."

"What are you talking about?"

"We saw you go into his house after the game the other night."

Ruth couldn't believe what she was hearing. She quickly shut the box and slid it back under her desk. She spoke to Shelby in a quiet but serious manner. "I will lose my job if they find out Ricky and I ever dated. It's a conflict of interest."

"You didn't do it, did you?" Shelby asked.

"Do what?" said Ruth.

"Set Ricky up. Steal his cap. Break his mirror." Shelby's mind ran through all the incidents.

"Of course not," Ruth said. "You thought I did all that?"

"Not really," said Angie. "We just couldn't figure out who else it could have been."

"Look," said Shelby. She pointed at one of the pictures on the table. It was a picture of Tom Van Ness at the marina posing by his boat.

"It's for an article I'm doing on Van Ness," Ruth said. "Why?"

Shelby pointed to the name of the boat—*Lucky Seven*. Shelby and Angie thought back to the boom box in the scoreboard. *Lucky 7* had been written on one of the speakers.

"Of course," said Shelby. "Van Ness wears number seven. He did all this to get Ricky off the team."

"And in two hours it looks like he's going to get his wish," said Angie. "We've got to stop this."

Shelby grabbed the phone and called Vince. Without even giving him a chance to say anything, she told him to meet her and Angie down at the marina.

"Do you mind filling me in, here?" asked Ruth.

"There's not really time right now," said Shelby. "But it will make a great article. First, though, you've got to get that announcement delayed. If Ricky gets traded, nothing else will matter."

Shelby and Angie raced down to the marina. As expected, Vince was there waiting for them. Much to their surprise, however, Scott Bushnell was with him.

Vince came over to Shelby. "You didn't let me talk," he said about the phone conversation. "Scott had come over to talk about Angie. He was there when you called and he asked to come along."

"You guys go check for the boat," said Angie. "I'll talk to Scott."

Shelby explained the situation to Vince while they tried to walk nonchalantly down the dock looking for *Lucky Seven*.

Angie, meanwhile, walked over to where Scott was standing. "I don't know how to say this, because I think you're a really great guy—"

"Don't worry," he interrupted. "Vince pretty much filled me in on how you feel. It's okay. I just wanted to come here and tell you face to face what I was trying to say in those notes."

Angie was surprised by his serious demeanor.

"I just wanted you to know that I've seen you around a lot." He stammered a little. "I think you're cool. I'm sure you'll make some guy a great girlfriend, even it that guy isn't me."

Suddenly it dawned on Angie. She was guilty of treating Scott the same way she hated being treated by other guys. She had disregarded him because he was a little offbeat. After all, the notes and flowers were charming when she thought Jerry had sent them. Why were they any less charming now?

"I don't know what Vince told you," said Angie, "but I'd love to go to Spring Fling with you."

Shelby and Vince, meanwhile, were sneaking onboard *Lucky Seven*.

"This may not be the stupidest thing we've done . . ." said Vince.

". . . but it's got to be in the top ten," answered Shelby.

If she could find the boom box, she would know for sure that Van Ness was guilty. They went down into the cabin, which was decorated in a baseball theme.

In a closet, Vince found several splintered bats.

"It's odd," said Shelby. "They've been partially cut through."

They didn't find the boom box, but they found something better—a weathered Red Sox cap. "Ricky Baines" was scrawled inside the bill.

"We've got him," said Shelby.

Just then they felt a slight jolt. It was the boat pulling away from the marina.

Chapter
12

Shelby and Vince tried not to panic. They weren't sure if they had been caught or if they were just in the wrong place at the wrong time.

It didn't take long to find out.

"Who are you?" Van Ness bellowed as he went into the cabin. "And what are you doing on my boat?"

The looked out the porthole and saw that they were in the middle of the Charles River. There was nowhere to run.

"Us?" answered Vince. "We're with the Coast Guard auxiliary. We're doing boat inspections."

"Yeah, right,'" said Van Ness. Then he recognized Shelby from the other night. "Are you with the press?"

"Not exactly," she said.

Van Ness noticed that they'd found Ricky's cap. He looked down at the broken bats.

"You haven't broken any laws yet," Shelby said. "But if you hurt us, you will."

Van Ness laughed. "I'm not going to hurt you."

"You're not?" said Vince.

"There's no reason to," he said.

Vince and Shelby weren't sure what was happening. "Then what are you going to do?" she asked.

"Watch television." He smiled and turned on the cabin television. "We'll just stay out here until they have the press conference and announce the trade. After that, it won't matter. Like you said, I didn't break any laws. And besides, once Ricky's gone, the team's going to need me in left field."

"How will you explain keeping us hostage?" Vince demanded.

"I won't have to," said Van Ness. "You're stowaways. I can tell them that I didn't even know you were on board."

Shelby and Vince were beaten. He blocked the exit from the cabin. And even if he hadn't, it would have been hard to swim to shore.

Suddenly the roar from a loudspeaker filled the air with noise. "This is Boston Maritime Police demanding that the occupants of *Lucky Seven* step out on to the deck of the boat."

Van Ness looked out and saw a marine patrol boat. A smiling Shelby and Vince did, too. Standing on the deck of the police boat were Angie and Scott.

Tom Van Ness was beaten.

It turns out that we were too late to stop the press conference from happening. Although Ruth did get to the general manager in time to tell him what was up. He stood before the members of the media to announce a major change on the team. But much to their surprise, he didn't announce that Ricky Baines had been traded. Instead, he told them that Tom Van Ness had decided to retire early because of an "unspecified family matter."

They didn't find out what that matter was until they read Ruth's column the next day. It doesn't look like Van Ness will be charged with a crime. He paid his price by losing out on the rest of the year's salary—approximately $1.4 million.

Bud Jenkins wasn't so lucky. An undercover police officer took him up on his offer to deliver an authentic Ricky Baines hat. The hat, of course, was a fake. By selling phony merchandise, Jenkins violated his court agreement and was forced to close down his business and serve sixty days in jail.

Perhaps the biggest change, though, was for Ruth. She told her editor all about her relationship with Ricky. She also told him that she had never shown any favoritism. Her series of critical articles was proof of that.

The editor was convinced that everything was on the up and up, so she was able to keep her job. She did, however, ask to be assigned the basketball beat, and now she's covering the Celtics instead of the Red Sox.

Spring Fling was great. Vince and I doubled with Angie and Scott. We had so much fun. Much to Angie's surprise, Scott was a perfect match for her. She helped him be a little more serious and he helped her loosen up a bit.

The four of us went out again, to a Red Sox game. Ricky had arranged for us to have box seats to show his appreciation. Ruth sat with us. It was the first time she'd sat with the "regular people" in a long time. The food wasn't as good, but we got to yell all we wanted.

I still don't know if I believe in luck or not. But when I look at the people around me and see how wonderful they are, I know that I certainly do feel lucky.

About the Author

JAMES PONTI has written for newspapers, magazines, television shows, and movies, including *The Mystery Files of Shelby Woo* television series since its first season. He lives in Winter Park, Florida, with his wife, Denise, and sons, Alex and Grayson. Like the characters in this story, he is a firm believer in the Curse of the Bambino. A lifelong fan of the Boston Red Sox, he holds as one of his favorite memories the night his mother woke him up after midnight to watch a replay of Carlton Fisk hitting a home run in the 1975 World Series.

NICKELODEON/MINSTREL BOOKS POINTS PROGRAM

Official Rules

1. *HOW TO COLLECT POINTS*

Points may be collected by purchasing any book with the special Minstrel®/Nickelodeon "Read Books, Earn Points, Get Stuff!" offer. Only books that bear the burst "Read Books, Earn Points, Get Stuff!" are eligible for the program. Points can be redeemed for merchandise by completing the coupons (found in the back of the books) and mailing with a check or money order in the exact amount to cover postage and handling to Minstrel Books/Nickelodeon Points Program, P.O. Box 7777-G140, Mt. Prospect, IL 60056-7777. Each coupon is worth points. (See individual book for point value.) Copies of coupons are not valid. Simon & Schuster is not responsible for lost, late, illegible, incomplete, stolen, postage-due, or misdirected mail.

2. *40 POINT MINIMUM*

Each redemption request must contain a minimum of 40 points in order to redeem for merchandise.

3. *ELIGIBILITY*

Open to legal residents of the United States (excluding Puerto Rico) and Canada (excluding Quebec) only. Void where taxed, licensed, restricted, or prohibited by law. Redemption requests from groups, clubs, or organizations will not be honored.

4. *DELIVERY*

Allow 6-8 weeks for delivery of merchandise.

5. *MERCHANDISE*

All merchandise is subject to availability and may be replaced with an item of merchandise of equal or greater value at the sole discretion of Simon & Schuster.

6. *ORDER DEADLINE*

All redemption requests must be received by January 31, 1999, or while supplies last. Offer may not be combined with any other promotional offer from Simon & Schuster. Employees and the immediate family members of such employees of Simon & Schuster, its parent company, subsidiaries, divisions and related companies and their respective agencies and agents are ineligible to participate.

COMPLETE THE COUPON AND MAIL TO
NICKELODEON/MINSTREL POINTS PROGRAM
P.O. BOX 7777-G140
MT. PROSPECT, IL 60056-7777

NICKELODEON
MINSTREL° BOOKS

NAME_____

ADDRESS_____

CITY _____ STATE _____ ZIP _____

THIS COUPON WORTH FIVE POINTS
Offer expires January 31, 1999

I have enclosed _____coupons and a check/money order (in U.S. currency only) made payable to "Nickelodeon/Minstrel Books Points Program" to cover postage and handling.

❏ 40–75 points (+ $3.50 postage and handling)

❏ 80 points or more (+ $5.50 postage and handling)

1464-01(2of2)

It's tough being the new kid on the planet!

THE JOURNEY OF ALLEN STRANGE™

Meet Allen Strange. He's a typical teenager trying to fit in at a new school...except Allen's an alien who was accidentally stranded on Earth. Now, with the help of his new friends, Robbie and Josh Stevenson, he's trying to find a way to get home—and to keep his special powers a secret!

Based on the hit series from Nickelodeon

Original stories available in January '99

A MINSTREL® BOOK

Published by Pocket Books

To find out more about The Journey of Allen Strange or any other Nickelodeon show, visit Nickelodeon Online on America Online (Keyword: NICK) or on the Web at nick.com.

2035-01